"You're obligated to serve as Caleb's nanny."

"So what are you going to do if I refuse?" Jake replied. "Sue me?"

"I—"

"Call the police?"

"Well—"

"Chain me up and drag me to your house?"

At the last question, Delaney couldn't have forced a sound from her throat if her life depended on it.

He inched closer than she would have ever thought possible with the table between them.

"Tell me, McBride. What would you do?"

But she couldn't think. She could barely manage to breathe as an image flashed through her head of a hot sultry night. And this man in chains.

Dear Reader,

This month, a new star comes out to shine as American Romance's "Rising Star" program continues. We've searched the heavens for the best new talent...and the best new stories.

I'm extremely delighted to introduce Lisa Bingham to American Romance. Though this is her first contemporary, she is the bestselling author of nine historical romances. Lisa was recently married and is currently refurbishing a farmhouse in northern Utah. Writing is her passion, and she enjoys the opportunities it gives her to meet new and fascinating people.

Turn the page and catch a "Rising Star"!

Sincerely,

Debra Matteucci
Senior Editor & Editorial Coordinator
Harlequin Books
300 E. 42nd St.
New York, NY 10017

Lisa Bingham

NANNY JAKE

Harlequin Books

TORONTO • NEW YORK • LONDON
AMSTERDAM • PARIS • SYDNEY • HAMBURG
STOCKHOLM • ATHENS • TOKYO • MILAN
MADRID • WARSAW • BUDAPEST • AUCKLAND

To Eddie the Barbarian—
It took a while,
but here's your cover.

ISBN 0-373-16602-8

NANNY JAKE

Copyright © 1995 by Lisa Bingham Rampton.

All rights reserved. Except for use in any review, the reproduction or utilization of this work in whole or in part in any form by any electronic, mechanical or other means, now known or hereafter invented, including xerography, photocopying and recording, or in any information storage or retrieval system, is forbidden without the written permission of the publisher, Harlequin Enterprises Limited, 225 Duncan Mill Road, Don Mills, Ontario, Canada M3B 3K9.

All characters in this book have no existence outside the imagination of the author and have no relation whatsoever to anyone bearing the same name or names. They are not even distantly inspired by any individual known or unknown to the author, and all incidents are pure invention.

This edition published by arrangement with Harlequin Books S.A.

® and TM are trademarks of the publisher. Trademarks indicated with ® are registered in the United States Patent and Trademark Office, the Canadian Trade Marks Office and in other countries.

Printed in U.S.A.

Chapter One

"Dr. McBride?" The voice on the telephone was punctuated by a burst of static.

"Yes, Linda. I'm still here."

Dr. Delaney McBride took the key to the ladies' rest room from the service-station attendant and nodded her thanks. Draping her dry-cleaning bag and her purse over her left arm and holding the phone with her right, she strode toward the back of the cinder block building, eager to exchange the chemical- and blood-spattered suit she wore for something fresh.

Only after reaching the relative privacy of the corridor did she allow herself a small grimace. Why hadn't the Fates been kind? Why hadn't some sixth sense warned her that she would spend most of her morning at the Lexington Institute trying to talk some deranged man out of a hostage situation over a sperm donation he'd made three years ago? Why hadn't she had an inkling that Mr. Willie Parker would begin throwing petri dishes and specimen cups against the wall in a fit of rage? If she'd had some clue, any kind of hint of what was to come, she wouldn't have worn her best white silk and heels. Of course, she thought with a slight sigh of irritation, if she'd had a hint of what was to come, she wouldn't be wearing her latest experiment, either.

"Doctor?"

"Go ahead, Linda." She hitched her shoulder a fraction of an inch higher to press the cellular phone tighter against her ear.

"I rescheduled all of your consultations at the other clinics, as you asked, but your calendar is strained for the next few weeks."

"That's fine." Delaney was accustomed to long hours of work. "Thank you for making the changes. This is the first minute I've had away from the police station after giving a statement."

"A few things have happened here that I thought you might want to know about. Dr. Braxton dropped by the lab. He wanted to inform you that the benefit dinner your mother organized on behalf of the Lexington Institute has been rescheduled to six weeks from next Friday. Judge Reinhold and Senator Wheeler will be there. They've specifically asked to be seated at the Prodigy's table."

"Fine." Delaney didn't even blink at the nickname her co-workers at the research institute had given her. Over ten years ago, at the ripe old age of nineteen, she'd earned a place on the board of directors of the Lexington Fertility and Research Institute. The job had afforded her instant notoriety, as well as a healthy dose of ribbing from her new colleagues. It had taken nearly a decade of hard work and determination, and a stoic sense of pride, to squelch some of the nicknames she'd been given. Of them all, the Prodigy was the least annoying.

"Tina Carruthers came to see you, as well. The reunion with your old sorority sisters is planned for the same night. She really wanted to speak to you. She said there was some sort of scandal with one of the other girls in the group. Evidently she's been charged with embezzlement."

"Embezzlement? You've got to be kidding."

"That's what she said. Tina seemed eager to talk to you about it, but she said she'd see you at the reunion if she didn't hear from you before then."

Delaney stifled a quick sigh. Deep down, if she dared admit the truth to herself, she knew she would much rather spend the evening with the women she'd once known in college than eat chicken à la Goodyear with her co-workers, but she couldn't possibly miss the benefit. "Call Tina and tell her I can't..." Offering a short sigh, she changed her mind. "No. I'll call. What else?"

"Have you prepared a statement for the press yet? They've been camping out in the corridor all afternoon trying to get a quote on the Willie Parker situation."

"Tell them I have no comment, then get security to move them away," Delaney said firmly. "I don't think any of our patients or sperm donors would be too thrilled by the lack of privacy."

Delaney let herself into the grease-smudged rest room and turned on the lights. The fluorescent tube overhead buzzed and flickered like a trapped moth as it fought to illuminate the cramped space. The door shut firmly behind her, enclosing her in a narrow cocoon of blessed solitude. From far away came the muted sound of a radio, the clicking of gas meters, the rattle of tools, but Delaney didn't care. Somehow, she had survived the afternoon from hell without her usual reserve cracking into a hundred pieces, and she was alone.

"Dr. McBride?"

No, not quite alone.

"Yes, Linda."

"There's also a . . . delivery here for you." Linda's voice grew strangely quiet, as if she were afraid of being overheard. "Were you expecting anything?"

"Only those samples from Atlanta."

"This is slightly . . . larger than a sperm sample, and I'd say a little more . . . personal in nature."

Personal? Delaney would be the first to admit she had no real personal life or interests outside the lab. Her work was all she needed, all she craved. "What is it?"

"Well, it's—"

There was a burst of static and some muffled conversation, as if Linda had covered the phone with her hand. Then, from far away, came a wailing noise. "I think you'd better get back here right away," she said quickly when she returned. "Evidently you need to accept this...package in person. He won't leave it with me. Also, you asked me to remind you of the tour with Dr. Van Klieg from the home office. You scheduled it for five."

Delaney glanced at the delicate gold watch strapped to her wrist, but the shattered crystal had stopped at half-past two. Judging by the traffic already beginning to gather, the afternoon commute was well under way. "What time is it now?"

"Four-thirty. You have barely a half hour to spare."

"I'll never make it in time. See if you can get in touch with Dr. Van Klieg or his assistant and reschedule. If not, have Burt Addleman take him on a tour of the facilities." She eased one arm out of her blood-spattered jacket, then the other, and began unbuttoning the cuffs of her blouse. "I'm changing my clothes now. With the rush-hour traffic I could be nearly forty-five minutes in transit."

"Anything else?"

"No. No, that's all. I know you'd planned to leave at five. If I'm not there, you may as well go home. I'll see you first thing tomorrow."

There was a long pause on the other end.

"You're sure?"

"I'm sure. I know you've got that Little League tournament at six. If the deliveryman refuses to leave the package without my signature, give him a soft drink and a magazine and tell him to wait in the reception area. There's no sense in your staying, too. There's nothing in the office or reception area he can steal, unless he wants to take a vial and force us to check a sperm sample for slow swimmers."

Another long pause. *"Nooo..."* Linda drawled. "I don't think that would prove at all necessary."

Delaney frowned at the odd comment, but merely added, "I'll see you tomorrow morning, then?"

"First thing," Linda said. It was as if there were some sort of hidden message in the agreement.

Shrugging at her secretary's unusual behavior, Delaney terminated the call and set the phone on the narrow metal shelf above the basin. Bending over the chipped porcelain sink, she splashed tepid water on her cheeks, then straightened, dabbing at the moisture with one of the rough paper towels provided. The lavatory mirror bolted to the wall had long since cracked. A crazed web of glass caused the face that looked back at her to buckle and shift in a most unflattering manner. Delaney blamed the effect on the mirror, as if the glaring light could be entirely responsible for the pallor of her skin and the hollows beneath her eyes.

She needed sleep. How long had it been—a week? Two? With all the work at the institute, then the Willie Parker crisis...she couldn't remember the last time she'd had one night of deep, uninterrupted rest. Instead, she tossed and turned, worried, and tossed some more.

Concerned, she bent a little closer to the largest unaffected portion of the mirror, peering critically at her own reflection. Tomorrow was her birthday. At exactly two minutes after noon, she would turn thirty. The big three-O. Did it show? Her skin was still clear, still soft, still stretched tightly over her bones—perhaps too tightly? Did she look too drawn? Too...*old?*

She felt old. But then, she'd felt old all her life. Probably one of the by-products of graduating from high school at the age of nine. Earning her first medical degree by fifteen. In the past, such an accomplishment had always instilled in her a sense of pride—as much at having survived all the boarding schools and the constant change, as at earning the degrees themselves. But today, the thought rang hollowly inside her head. With so many accomplishments behind her, what was left for her to do now?

At thirty.

Middle age creeping up on her.

Stepping back, Delaney tipped her face to the light and eyed the smooth sweep of russet hair coiled against her nape, the elegant silk suit. As always, she looked professional, brilliant, successful...and very staid. Sighing, she realized her life had become as sterile as the lab where she spent most of her time. But what could she do? She was pleased with all the research she'd done; she knew there were hundreds of women who would trade places with her in a heartbeat.

So why did she keep thinking that there was something missing?

As soon as the thought entered her head, she thrust it away. Nonsense. She was simply allowing the mores of a youth-based society to influence her thinking. She should remember that in *her* chosen profession, she was still considered a youngster in comparison to those with whom she worked.

Lifting her purse onto the edge of the sink, she withdrew containers of cosmetics, finishing powder and hair spray. Employing an artist's skill, she repaired the evidence of the stressful afternoon. Once her makeup had been restored, she stripped the rest of her stained suit away and exchanged the pieces for the one she'd retrieved from the cleaners early that morning. Completely dressed, she hung the soiled garments on the hanger with meticulous care. Ruined. The suit was utterly ruined.

She hesitated only a moment before tearing the clothes free, wadding them in a ball and stuffing them in the trash. Grabbing her purse and the mobile phone, she exited the bathroom, head held high. After returning the key to the attendant, she slid into the forest green Jaguar she'd left parked by the ice machine and automatically tucked the phone in its cradle beneath the dash. With a little luck, she could be back at the research facilities nearly on schedule.

She might even be able to catch up with Van Klieg's tour, if he'd decided to have Burt show him around.

Forty minutes later, Delaney pulled into a parking place adjacent to the wing that housed her private offices at the Lexington Institute. Clipping her security card to her collar, Delaney eased from the car, damning the blast of hot May air that made it feel a good deal more like July.

Locking the car doors behind her, she marched down the sidewalk, searching the area for some sort of delivery van or truck, hoping it would provide a clue to the mysterious package. It irritated her that she had to worry about such a thing when she should be checking on Van Klieg, but Linda had been so odd on the phone. So secretive. After all, it could simply be some ridiculous birthday present from her parents.

But her parents had already sent her a year's subscription to Granny Goodall's Goody of the Week Club.

Maybe it was a sales pitch from a pharmaceutical company.

Unlikely.

Those samples from Atlanta.

Highly improbable, if Linda was to be believed.

Then what? What would demand her immediate attention on a day like today?

With each step, she became a little more frustrated, a little more angry. It wasn't until she was climbing the steps to her office door that the tiny hairs at the back of her neck prickled slightly, warning her that she was being observed.

Turning, she saw that a man sat in the shade pooled beneath the trees surrounding the outdoor eating area. He grasped a toddling youngster by the hand to keep him from wandering away, but he was staring overtly at her.

Delaney twisted away from his scrutiny, sliding her key card through the security lock, but the intensity of his gaze soon caused her to peer at him again.

In the past, she had prided herself on being a woman who could remain unimpressed by athletic males—those who were trim, lithe and well-muscled. But this time, she couldn't drag her gaze away. There was something about him. Something that set her inner alarms jangling. In an instant, she knew that he was the type that was immediately, gut-wrenchingly appealing to all women—even her. It took only a glance for her to feel certain that this man was bad—very, very bad—and that no self-respecting woman should admit she was attracted to the type. It was there in his eyes. His posture.

Even as the thought flashed through her head, the stranger rose to his feet, slinging a mesh bag stuffed with toys over his shoulder before scooping the child into his arms. Delaney was struck motionless by the odd combination—the overtly masculine devil-in-denim male, carrying a little boy and his toys. A breeze pushed the white T-shirt against the man's torso, revealing a washboard stomach and drawing her attention to a strong set of legs poured into a hankie-soft pair of old jeans. His powerful arms seemed capable of crushing the toddler, yet remained incredibly gentle.

The key card slipped from her fingers, and Delaney swore under her breath. What in the world had come over her? Embarrassed by her own actions, she bent to pick up the card, hoping that the action would give her time to gather her scattered wits. Unfortunately, her plan backfired, because the man stopped only a few feet away. From her vantage point two steps above him, her gaze landed on the white-blue patch of denim that cupped his crotch. There was a slight bit of fraying there. Near his fly. As if the fabric would soon—

Stop it! a little voice in her head interrupted frantically.

Clutching the key card as if it were a talisman, she briefly squeezed her lashes closed. *Get control of yourself,* she silently told herself, gathering the calm, the reserve, the poise, that she'd developed over the years. But the objective was not that easily obtained. For the first time in months—years—she was seeing a member of the opposite sex as something other than a research project.

Once again, her gaze strayed to that tiny patch of worn-out denim and bounced guiltily away. *As if you could look at this stranger in a clinical way,* the inner voice said mockingly. She'd never seen anyone like this at the institute. Although there were no out-

ward physical traits that could be attributed to im-
potence or infertility, she doubted very much that
this man suffered from such problems. The testos-
terone all but throbbed in the air around him.

Straightening, she pushed the door to her suite of
offices open and stepped into the cool, air-conditioned depths of the waiting room.

Business. Get your mind back to business.

Remembering why she had come to her offices in
the first place, she searched the quiet waiting room
for some sign of a deliveryman, but the room was
empty. Blast. That meant that her curiosity about the
mysterious package would not be satisfied tonight.

"Ms. McBride?"

She whirled, a hand going to her throat, at the
sound of a deep male voice. The door had not swung
closed behind her, as she'd assumed. Instead, the
stranger she'd so blatantly stared at had followed her
into the building.

Delaney frowned in disapproval at his presump-
tuous attitude. He'd better not be a member of the
press. Her gaze skipped to the child. She'd heard of
a few unethical ways to get an interview, but using a
baby to gain entrance to a fertility clinic was, in her
opinion, about as low as a person could go.

"Yes?" Her suspicions gave her tone a hard edge.

The man didn't speak right away, making her feel
inexplicably uncomfortable and fidgety. A frown
appeared between his brows, and he seemed to be

studying her quite intently, as if measuring her character in a single glance.

"Don't you think it was a little careless of you to wait until now before coming back?" he finally asked. "What if I hadn't been able to stay?"

The unexpected verbal attack caused Delaney's jaw to drop ever so slightly.

"Excuse me?"

He didn't speak again, just waited expectantly. The baby in his arms must have sensed some of the tension radiated by the man, because he began to fuss. He quieted it by bouncing the boy in his arms.

"Do I know you?" she finally asked, although the question was idiotic. This was not the sort of man anyone would forget.

"I'm Jacob," he said, his lips tipping in a faint smile. "Jacob Turk. But everyone calls me Jake."

He held out his free hand for her to shake and, still confused, she allowed her own to be swallowed by his, gripped with strong, faintly callused fingers.

"You're different from what I expected," he stated.

"Oh?" she offered weakly, wondering if this was some sort of test.

"The description I was given was a little off the mark. But then, I thought you'd be older, too."

Older.

Old.

Thirty.

When she didn't offer any kind of response, the man released her hand, combing his hair away from his forehead with his fingers. For the first time, Delaney noted that the dark waves were much longer than she had supposed. Because of his impressive height, she could just manage to see that the ebony strands had been drawn to the back of his neck, then plaited in a thick braid that fell between his shoulder blades.

Oh, yes. This man was the sort who could be *very* bad. Not at all like those she was used to conversing with—elegant businessmen, with their leather briefcases, or obsessive scientists, with their starched lab coats.

The pause in the conversation became incredibly long and incredibly uncomfortable. The toddler squirmed to get down, lunging against the tight handhold the man kept, but Jake held him firm, and finally broke the silence.

"Look, you *are* Delaney McBride, aren't you?" He scoured her form from head to toe with his eyes.

"Yes."

"Marlene told you I was coming today at four, didn't she?"

"Marlene?" Try as she might, she couldn't seem to piece together the reasons for this man being here, at her office, with a baby on his hip. Nor could she fathom why he should be so irritated with her. "Marlene who?"

"Marlene Detry."

She shook her head in confusion. "I'm afraid I don't... know anyone..." Her words trailed away, and she looked more closely at the baby in the man's arms. "*Marlie* Detry?" As far as Delaney knew, no one had ever called the effervescent girl she had known in college anything but Marlie.

He nodded.

"But I haven't seen her for ages."

Marlie Detry had been one of her sorority sisters. She'd come to Delaney some time before, upset, pregnant, and asking if Delaney knew of anyone who might be interested in the private adoption of her baby. Delaney had given her a few names of reputable lawyers who handled such cases, but Marlie had called some time later to announce the birth of her son and explain that she'd changed her mind about adoption. Apart from that, Delaney hadn't had much contact at all with the woman. Even in college, they'd never been close.

Jake gestured to the baby in his arms. "She said you were there when Caleb was born."

"No. Although I did visit her in the hospital a day or so after the birth."

"But you haven't seen her since?"

"No."

"Even though you were named Caleb's godmother?"

"*Godmother?*" The word nearly stuck in her throat. A sick suspicion began to settle into her stomach. "Mr. Turk, why exactly are you here?"

His eyes narrowed, as if he didn't quite believe she'd asked the question. "Marlene told me to bring the baby to you. She's been indicted for embezzlement. Two days ago, she skipped bail, leaving instructions that—if all went well—you were going to be in charge of Caleb from now on."

Chapter Two

Delaney McBride hadn't known he was coming today.

Jacob recognized that fact the same instant an expression of shock slipped over her features. Dammit all to hell! Didn't Marlene have any sense? Hadn't she even bothered to inform this woman about her plans for Caleb before running from the law?

But even as the questions shot through his brain, Jake knew the answer. *No.* Marlene had simply dumped her boy in another person's lap and gone on her merry way, leaving all the details to her lawyer, never once thinking that there might be some kind of problem with the arrangement, or that Delaney McBride wouldn't *want* to take her son.

He clenched his jaw in an effort to keep the expletives racing through his mind from bursting free. What a mess. What an absolute mess!

He quickly surveyed the woman who stood pale and stunned in front of him. He noted the expensive linen suit—carefully pressed, even in this heat—the faultless silk shirt, the elegant leather pumps, and he knew in an instant why Marlie had thought Ms. McBride would make a perfect mother for her boy. Just looking at Delaney McBride, Jake could see that she was a woman accustomed to order, schedules, lists. That was one area where Marlie had never excelled. She'd always been flighty and prone to impulsiveness. That was a fact that had made motherhood especially difficult for a woman accustomed to travel and parties and freedom. She'd never grasped the fact that Caleb needed constant feeding and changing and educating. That he couldn't be left in a corner to entertain himself.

Jake should never have brought him here—he should have insisted the boy be given to him without the two-month trial period Marlene had insisted Delaney be given. But from the way Marlene spoke, he'd thought that Delaney McBride was some kind, understanding grandmotherly woman in support hose. He'd thought the arrangements would work out for the best and give him a little time to deal with the transfer he would be making to a new job. Now he was just pummeled by more doubts.

"Mr. . . ."

"Turk."

"Mr. Turk." He saw McBride straighten and stiffen by degrees, as if she were calling upon all her inner resources of calm. "I really don't understand what's going on here, but I can assure you that there's obviously been a mistake. I am *not* this boy's godmother.''

''For the next two months, you're the guardian of record. If, after several visits from Marlie's lawyer, you are considered a suitable caregiver, you will be awarded permanent custody of the boy. If not, other arrangements have been made.''

''But—''

''Marlene had all the legal papers prepared that allow you to serve as the boy's guardian until then.''

''But that's absurd! I can't possibly... I mean, I wouldn't know the slightest... I...''

Her cheeks grew pink as she looked from Jake to the boy, then back again. It was a curious reaction. One that made her seem slightly more vulnerable. A little younger. Quite a bit younger.

Jake didn't want to admit it, but he found himself becoming intrigued by her discomfiture. It somehow shifted the cool mask this woman had adopted at his arrival. Unfortunately, he knew he didn't have the time to dwell on such things.

''Look, Ms. McBride, I sympathize with your confusion, really I do.'' He glanced at his watch, feeling the press of time. He didn't want to abandon Caleb with this woman, but he'd already delayed leaving as long as he could. He had a business meeting at six with a group of corporate lawyers who were arranging the acquisition of some artwork Jake held, and he had to be at his second job by seven-thirty. He couldn't be late. He would have to sort all this out another day.

He looped his thumb around the strap of the diaper bag, transferring it to her shoulder, then lifted Caleb into her arms. She took the boy as a matter of reflex, but the child looked awkward and ill at ease in her grip, eyeing Jake with what appeared to be a mixture of confusion and dread.

Jacob had to steel himself against the boy's unspoken appeal for help. Two months. Just two months. Then, if McBride failed her motherhood test, Caleb would be his. Legally, morally, and in every other way possible.

Not wanting to delve too far into the future this early in the game, Jake said quickly, "In the bag you'll find diapers, toys and crackers. I've also included a change of clothing, some rompers, and a bunny suit."

"Bunny suit?" Delaney echoed weakly.

It was clear she had no idea what he meant, but he didn't bother to explain. She was a woman. No doubt the instincts for nurturing that were missing from Marlene's nature could help this woman find the footed pajamas when she needed them.

"The legal documents giving you custody are in a large manila envelope in the side pocket. Marlene also left a number where a message could be left for her in Paraguay...."

"Paraguay?"

"...but she won't be checking with her friends there until sometime tomorrow morning, so you're on your own tonight. I would stay and help, but Ms. Detry terminated my services as of last week, and I've got to get crosstown in—" he glanced at his watch again "—thirty minutes."

"But..."

"Look, Ms. McBride, I'm sorry about all this." He glanced at Caleb, who was sucking two fingers on his left hand in confusion. "I'm more sorry than you'll ever know." He said more to himself this time. For the next two months he had no legal rights to the boy. That was a fact he'd had to drum into his head time and time again these past few days.

"I'll check back with you tomorrow to arrange the delivery of the crib and high chair. Marlene didn't have your home address."

"But..." She stared at him the way a drowning man might watch a drifting life preserver. It was then that he noticed that her eyes were really quite lovely. Large, thickly lashed, and a curious mixture of blue, brown and gold. "But I don't know anything about this child!"

"You'll learn. Trust me. Caleb has a mind of his own and isn't afraid to use it." Once again, Jake's brain prodded him to go, but he found himself rooted to the floor, offering needless instructions. "Be careful what you feed him. He hates spinach and carrots and loves bananas. Don't give him spaghetti, or you'll be wearing it. Try not to offer him fruit juice just before bed—and he's allergic to strawberries. I've left a list of instructions and a short medical history in a notebook next to his tub toys."

"Tub toys..."

He tickled Caleb under the boy's pudgy chin, trying to stifle the regrets that continued to pummel him. He shouldn't leave him here. He should take Caleb home.

But Jake knew that wasn't really an option. Without legal guardianship, he didn't have a hope in hell of keeping Caleb for more than a day or two. Besides which, Jake was staying with his brother, since Marlene had kicked him out of his rooms.

Turning on his heel, he strode purposefully to the door, knowing that he had to leave. Now.

"Mr. Turk!"

He paused, one hand on the knob. She was jiggling the baby awkwardly, a motion that was causing Caleb's face to screw up in preparation for an unholy scream. Jake had seen that look often enough to know what it preceded.

"Mr. Turk... who are you, exactly?"

Jake took one last look at the little boy. "I am... *was*... Caleb's nanny."

He stood still, silent, waiting for the reaction he was used to receiving upon such an announcement. The patent disbelief. He'd seen it a million times. True, he didn't look the part. But after a rebellious adolescence and an adventurous youth, he'd decided long ago that he didn't care what people thought. He liked kids. Liked them a lot. And he was good at what he did. He had over a decade of experience, as well as references from some of the wealthiest and most influential families in the country, to prove it.

To her credit, McBride didn't apologize for her reaction. Stepping forward, she regarded him in confusion—as if she'd heard him incorrectly.

"You're his nanny?" She spoke so softly that he almost didn't catch the words.

"Yes. I was. But for the next two months, he's your responsibility."

Turning his back on the boy and the rapport they'd formed, he walked out into the hot Los Angeles evening.

DELANEY WATCHED HIM GO, her mouth agape, her thoughts swirling in confusion. He couldn't leave. Not yet. Not like this. Dumping the diaper bag on the floor, she ran after him, but by the time she reached the parking lot, there was nothing to be seen but a red Jeep speeding away.

Caleb must have recognized the vehicle. He rubbed his fist against his nose, making a snuffling sound, then a sob.

"Shh... Shhh... Don't cry."

If Caleb understood, he didn't respond. The farther the Jeep drove through the parking lot, the more upset he grew, until he was screaming so loud, she feared he was having some sort of fit.

"No, baby, no," she mumbled, at a loss as to what to say to a— Good grief! She didn't even know how old the child was. When had she visited Marlene in the hospital? April? October? Had it been this year? Last? She couldn't remember. She'd been so busy. She'd stopped by to see Marlie only for a minute—as a courtesy.

Waaaagh!

"Hush, Caleb, hush."

But the child could not be consoled. He kept staring at the place where the Jeep had last been seen, his arms outstretched in supplication, his face growing red and shiny with perspiration and tears.

At any other moment, on any other day, Delaney might have summoned up the wherewithal to figure out what to do. But after having Willie Parker hold hostages until his sperm samples were returned and spending the whole afternoon with the culprit and the LAPD, she found her brain was behaving in an entirely sluggish manner.

"Ake! Na-nee Ake," the little boy began to chant between screams. "Ake!" His fingers opened and closed as if he could will the man to come back.

Delaney could truly empathize with the little boy's plight. She herself would have given anything to see Jake Turk turn his red Jeep around and come screeching back.

But he didn't. Even though she waited for him to do just that.

It was some time later, as a rivulet of sweat coursed down her back, that Delaney realized she would have to find some other means of dealing with the situation.

BORROWING A CAR SEAT from the company day-care center, she made her way home, letting herself into the cool confines of her home in Beverly Hills.

Long ago, the vaulting castlelike structure had been built by a silent-screen star. Her parents—who never ceased to dote on their only child—had bought it for her just after her twenty-fifth birthday. Delaney supposed it had been their way of encouraging her to begin "nesting" in one way or another. They'd hoped she would find a nice man, settle down and provide them with grandchildren. Unfortunately, the plan had backfired. Except for a few scattered pieces of furniture, Delaney had never really found the time to decorate the place.

Setting Caleb on the floor of the informal living room and dumping his toys in front of him, she prayed that he would be distracted long enough for her to use the phone. The moment she entered the house, she'd known just what to do. She would call her mother. Dodie McBride would know how to handle the situation! She might even volunteer to take the child for a few days to get all those grandmother-wannabe feelings out of her system.

Strengthened by purpose, Delaney sank onto a ladder-back chair and reached for the phone, which was resting on a pile of old telephone books. Caleb took one look at her, his lip trembling, then began to cry again, throwing himself down on the carpet in ultimate sorrow.

Frantically Delaney punched in the number to her parents' home.

After twelve rings, the phone was finally answered.

"Allo."

She squeezed her eyes shut, realizing that it was not Dodie McBride who'd answered, but her Haitian maid.

"Liato, is my mother there?"

"Not home."

"Where is she?"

"Not home."

"When will she *be* home?"

"When moth fly free in jungle."

Delaney pressed a finger to her aching temple. Caleb screamed even louder.

"Do you mean she has a committee meeting?" Delaney asked, raising her voice to be heard. Dodie McBride was forever involving herself in whatever eccentric causes she felt deserved her time, attention and money.

"Yes, ma'am. At meeting."

"For what?"

"Amazon butter-winged moth."

"The Amazon butter-winged moth," Delaney repeated in disbelief.

"I go now."

"No, Liato, wait, I—" But the woman had already hung up.

Delaney took one look at the boy screaming and crying on her floor and nearly wept herself.

What was she going to do?

The phone in her lap rang, making her jump. Quickly answering, she prayed it was Dodie, that she hadn't really been at some committee meeting.

"Delaney?"

The familiar voice of her old roommate, Tina Carruthers, caused her hopes to sink.

"Hi, Tina. I was going to call you."

"I know, I know, but I couldn't wait for you to find time in that schedule of yours." She rushed on without giving Delaney a chance to speak. "Have you heard about Marlie Detry?"

"Yes." Delaney sighed, rubbing the ache centered between her eyes.

"Oh." It was clear that Tina had wanted to convey the titillating details herself. "I hear she's gone to Brazil or something."

"Paraguay," Delaney said automatically.

"Oh, really?"

"Mmm..."

"Is that a child I hear crying and carrying on?" Tina asked.

"Umm...yes, it's...umm...it's my neighbor's son. I'm just watching him for an hour. Some emergency came up." Delaney didn't like having to lie, but she wasn't sure what else to do.

Caleb was beginning to wind down from his tantrum. He rolled to his back and glared at her, his face shiny with tears, his nose running, one hand held out in supplication, clenching and unclenching.

It was enough to break her heart.

Tina began chattering away on the other end of the line, talking about the reunion, the old days, the other sorority sisters, but Delaney didn't really listen. She was staring at the boy at her feet, remembering the times in her own childhood when she'd felt abandoned. She'd been an adult before she realized that when her parents left her at boarding schools and college dormitories, they'd suffered from the separation as much as she. At the time she'd thought they cared more about her schooling than about her feelings. Now she understood that they'd been at a loss as to how to handle her brilliance. They'd wanted to keep her near them, but they'd also wanted her to have the best teachers, the best education.

Would Caleb grow to understand why Marlie had brought him to a stranger? Would he even remember this day? The uncertainty of his future?

"Tina, I've got to go," she said, interrupting her.

There was a curious silence on the other end.

"Someone's here," Delaney explained absently. "I've got a business engagement the same evening as the reunion dinner you've planned, but I promise to call you soon for lunch."

"Well, if you're—"

"Bye."

Replacing the phone on its cradle, Delaney sank to the floor, reaching out a hesitant hand and wiping the moist curls away from Caleb's forehead.

"I'll try to make you feel safe with me, Caleb," she whispered.

His chin trembled, and he began to cry again. Pulling him close, Delaney wondered if he'd somehow comprehended what she was trying to say to him with such a statement.

Probably not.

She wasn't really sure herself.

"No, PLEASE! Don't put me on hold again!"

Delaney sighed when a medley of the finest elevator music reverberated in her ear. So far, she had been entertained with Brahms's "Lullaby," "Angel Baby," "Itsy Bitsy Spider," and her personal favorite, the Barney song. "I love you, you love me...." If she didn't get a real person with a real voice soon, she feared, she was going to scream.

"Na-nee Ake... Na-nee Ake..." Caleb's sweaty head was cradled next to her neck. He was nearly asleep, after having cried for three hours straight, but every time she moved or tried to put him down, he would wake up and begin to sob again. His grief was heart-wrenching, but Delaney's sympathy was quickly being crowded out by her own frustration and frazzled nerves—not to mention the aches in her arms, her legs, her back, her temples.

"Hellooo..." a voice on the other end called.

"Yes, I—"

"Please hooold. Only a little minute longer."

"No, I—"

The music returned. This time it sounded suspiciously like the Vienna Boys' Choir singing "She's Having My Baby."

"No, please don't do this to me," Delaney moaned in frustration. Caleb made a snuffling noise, and she tried to increase the rocking motion of her body, even as her muscles screamed in protest.

So far, she'd been through this same telephone procedure with Social Services, her lawyer, three temp agencies and two companies that provided nannies. She really wasn't in the mood to do it all again.

"Hello? Smythe and Eddington Child Care Placement Services. May I help you?"

Delaney hesitated ever so slightly, waiting for the music to return, but when the pause on the other end of the line grew quite long, she realized she actually had someone's attention.

"Yes. Yes!" Delaney said, tucking the receiver against her jaw and praying that little Caleb wouldn't be roused by the note of desperation in her tone. "I'm afraid I have a problem. This afternoon, a child was left at my office."

"You'll need to contact Social Services and—"

"No, I've contacted them. They've already told me that since I'm the legal guardian—"

"Of whom?"

"Little Caleb...the baby."

"Well, then, I suppose you've got yourself a new little boy. How wonderful!"

"No, no, you don't understand. I've never had children before. I don't know how to take care of him."

"So you need some help this evening. A reputable nanny."

"Yes!"

"I'm afraid we handle long-term relationships. You'll need to call a temp agency and—"

"No! I've already called *three* temp agencies. No one's available this evening."

"I'm so sorry. I'm afraid we're a bust, too." The woman chuckled at her own little private joke. "Even if you were contemplating a permanent arrangement, most of our nannies have waiting lists for months in advance."

Delaney sighed. "Yes, I'm familiar with that problem. I already called Wilmington Nannies, and Nanny, Inc."

"Oh...I see." It was clear that Delaney had offended the woman by putting this particular company so far down her list of contacts.

"Look, I'm afraid you've misunderstood me again," Delaney said. "I'm looking for one nanny in particular. A Mr. Jacob Turk."

"Oh, my, yes! Mr. Turk."

"Then he's with your agency?"

"Yes, indeed! Mr. Turk is one of our most highly rated caregivers. He's been with us for a dozen years. His references include the Abbingtons of Beverly Hills, the Wallaces of Bel Air, ex-Governor Pembroke and, of course, the Smythes and the Eddingtons."

"Of course," Delaney echoed weakly. At the sound of Jake's name, Caleb had begun to stir.

"Why, you must be Caleb Detry's new guardian!" the woman exclaimed in that too-happy voice that was beginning to eat away at Delaney's patience.

"I must?"

"Mr. Turk spoke of the boy most highly when he last visited our office. It's a shame that Ms. Detry had to... leave the country so suddenly."

"I couldn't agree more," Delaney said, with more feeling than she had intended.

"How can I help you, Ms.—?"

"Dr. McBride."

"*Doctor!* How lovely."

"Yes, well, I was wondering if you could put me in touch with Mr. Turk. This evening. It's quite important."

"You mean he's not there with the boy?"

"No."

"Oh, my. I wonder if Ms. Detry failed to inform him that she decided *against* terminating the six weeks he had left on his contract."

Delaney blinked. "I beg your pardon?"

"Well, you see, originally, Ms. Detry had paid for his services through the first week in July—this was before her unfortunate indictment. She called one of our associates to arrange a termination of the agreement and a partial refund, but then decided that you might wish to have Mr. Turk stay on for a week or two. Just until Caleb settled in."

"I see." For the first time in hours, Delaney was beginning to see a small sliver of hope somewhere in the distance.

"Of course, she may not have told Mr. Turk that she changed her mind." There was a gasp. "Oh, my! I hope not."

"Why is that?"

"Well, dear, according to his contract, he would have to give you a three-week notice to break things off from his end of the arrangement, which means that if he's made other plans for employment, he could be in quite a pickle."

"You mean serving as a nanny with someone else?"

"Oh, my, no. I don't think that would happen." The woman made a *tsk*ing noise. "You see, Mr. Turk would inform us first in such an instance. But as things stand, Mr. Turk left explicit instructions not to give him a new posting for some time. I believe he's going into some new line of work as a bit of a rest. We nannies sometimes need our holidays, too, you know. Even the best of us."

"I'm sure that's true—"

"Even if he were planning on signing on with another family again soon, there's a list," the woman said, interrupting Delaney. "Especially for Mr. Turk."

"Yes, I'm sure there is. I wonder if you could give me Mr. Turk's address, or his phone number? He arranged to see me tomorrow, but I must get in touch with him as soon as possible."

There was a heavy pause. "Oh, no. No, no, no." The woman clucked. "I'm so sorry, but it is strictly against company policy to release personal information about our clients."

"I know, but it's an emergency."

"What kind of emergency?"

Delaney opened her mouth and paused. She had to make this sound good, and she knew it. One false answer, and she'd be forced to listen to more Barney.

"The medicine he sent for Caleb's ears..."

"Yeess," the woman drawled, quite suspiciously.

"The label is missing. I don't know the dosage."

"But you're a doctor."

Drat. "I'm not *that* kind of doctor."

"Oh."

"I'm a doctor of science. Research." A little white lie, since Delaney had a medical degree in general practice, as well.

"Oh." Her explanation must have calmed the woman's fears, because she heard the click of computer keys somewhere in the background. Perhaps, at hearing her claim to be a scientist, the woman was ready to overlook her behavior due to the stereotypical response most people had to Delaney's work. She was often regarded as little more than an automaton or an absentminded scholar.

"Here it is." There was another pause, punctuated by several *hmm*s and *uh-huh*s, then she finally said, "I don't think Mr. Turk would like me to give out his unlisted number, but I suppose I could give you the address of his temporary residence."

"That would be wonderful." The woman on the other end had no idea how wonderful it would be.

"Do you have a pen, dear?"

Delaney snatched up the one lying on her desk.

"Yes, ma'am. I do."

Chapter Three

On a scale of one to ten, with ten being as lousy as it could get, Jacob Turk's day had scored a twenty-seven.

Jake sighed, pulling the leather thong from his hair and combing the strands free with his fingers. Stretching the cramped muscles of his arms and chest, he weaved his way along a familiar path through the maze of harshly lit halls that led from the inner offices of Safety and Security to the rear employee parking lot. As he stepped outside, he winced when the relentless evening heat settled around him like a heavy wool blanket. More out of habit than from a conscious awareness of his actions, he threw his gym bag on the passenger seat of his Jeep, gunned the engine and drove through the private gates of the Twin Towers theme park.

The Mardi Gras-colored lights behind him had barely faded from his rearview mirror before Jake was forced to admit that his mind wasn't really focused on his driving, or his bad day at work. He was thinking of Caleb—and the stiff-backed, slender, hazel-eyed woman who'd been given the right to keep him for a few weeks.

Jake had been rude to her earlier that day—too rude. But even after all the years he'd worked as a nanny, there had been something special about the bond he'd formed with Caleb. Maybe it was the fact that the little boy had been the first infant Jake cared for. Because of his size and stern manner, Jake's jobs usually involved older children or wayward teens.

But Caleb...

The little boy had wrapped his fingers around Jake's heart, and it wasn't easy letting go. Taking the toddler to Ms. McBride, he'd felt as if someone had ordered him to surrender his own son. Dangerous emotions, considering his predicament, but real nonetheless.

All day, Jake had tried to ease the unaccustomed sense of loss by thinking about the path his own future was taking. He'd never done anything the easy way. As an adolescent, he'd dropped out of high school, joined a biker gang for a year, and learned the hard way the value of an education. Taking a job as a live-in companion to a wayward thirteen-year-old boy, Jake had put himself through night school—for a secondary school diploma first, then a college degree, then a master's. And, through it all, he'd fought to play by his own rules, to do things his way.

It had been the only true path to happiness, as far as he was concerned.

Until Caleb.

Damn Marlene Detry, anyway, he thought suddenly. He didn't know why she'd insisted on playing these games. For months, knowing the indictment was forthcoming, she'd dithered about what to do with Caleb. With no family of her own, she'd vacillated between giving the boy to Jake and providing him with a mother. A real mother. She'd been obsessed with the idea. And then there was the fact that she thought Jake was a little too rough around the edges, a little too rebellious when it came to society's expectations. Jake could only be glad that she'd followed her lawyer's advice and insisted on a trial period for Delaney McBride. Two months. Ms. McBride had two months to prove she would be a fit mother. If not, Caleb would be returned to Jake. Permanently.

Of course, not in his wildest dreams had Jake thought that Marlene would have forgotten to inform McBride of the entire situation.

Hell. She would have to be told.

But then again, she would probably be relieved. She hadn't looked as if she wanted the boy, anyway. She was so far from Marlene's idea of Supermom that it wasn't even funny. She was much too...rigid, too...repressed. As if she'd spent her whole life encased in ice and needed a good melting about now—

something he wouldn't have minded doing, if they'd met any other way.

The thought came like a bolt of lightning, taking him by such surprise that he missed a gear. Swearing again, Jake immediately shoved that idea from his head, but it was galling to admit that, had she been an old woman in support hose, he might have made arrangements to see Caleb tonight, just to make sure he'd settled in. He might have helped her adjust to the sudden arrival of a baby in the house. But not with *that* woman. She was all wrong for Caleb. *All* wrong.

A gust of tepid air slid over Jake's skin as he brought his Jeep to a stop in the drive of the simple postwar dwelling he shared with Nick. Stepping onto the driveway, he grabbed his gym bag, wincing when he pulled the sore muscles spanning his torso. Only an hour before, he'd been smacked in the ribs with a six-foot broadsword. His body wasn't being very forgiving about the day's work, and it was especially irritating because the injury had resulted from his own inability to concentrate.

Chalk up another point against that McBride woman. In a single encounter, she had managed to infect his brain. Even now, he could remember the dark sweep of her hair—and those huge hazel eyes that seemed to peer deep into his soul. He couldn't let go of the fact that if he'd met her at some other time, in some other circumstances, he would have taken more than a second glance.

The keys jingled in Jacob's hand as he moved up the cracked walk that led to the front door. Judging by the absence of lights and the lateness of the hour, Nick was either working late or had persuaded one of his fellow employees to go out for a beer after his shift. Jake would have put his money on the latter. And he'd have bet a month's pay that the co-worker was none other than the lovely Maryann DuBois, marketing director.

Go get 'em, Nick, Jacob urged silently. At least one of them was having a good day.

Too late, a rustling noise warned him that he wasn't alone. Pausing in midstride, Jake squinted at the feminine shape sitting on the porch, her back so straight she could have had a fireplace poker for a spine.

"Mr. Turk."

The greeting slid out of the darkness.

"McBride?" Her name burst from his lips before he could stop it.

"Yes."

"I'll be damned." Then he added, somewhat inhospitably, "What are you doing here?"

His eyes bounced from her to Caleb, who was curled up in a blanket on the porch swing, obviously exhausted.

Delaney rose from her perch on the stoop, the movement rife with her obvious will to keep calm. Those thickly lashed hazel eyes sent her gaze from his head to his toes, making him aware that he'd changed into a pair of gym shorts and a tank top after work. His hair waved untidily over his shoulders and down his back—and he'd have bet, from the way her gaze clung a little longer than necessary, that his skin still retained a healthy portion of baby oil.

"I think we should talk." Her chin rose to a prouder angle.

"About what?"

"Caleb."

"What's wrong?"

She waved dismissively. "Nothing. Everything." She sighed and then admitted, "He's been crying for you all evening."

Jake had to steel himself against that news.

"Who told you where to find me?"

"The agency."

"They aren't supposed to give out my address."

"Why not? Since you are now in my employ?"

"What?"

Bending, she retrieved a document from her handbag and held it out to him. After glancing at the heading, he didn't really need to study it further. "If you're referring to my working arrangements with Marlene, then I'm afraid you're out of luck. She terminated my services as of this week."

"No, Mr. Turk. She did not." She flipped a page, then pointed to a paragraph she had underlined. "According to this agreement, you are still Caleb's nanny—providing that I agree to continue paying your salary until such time as you give me three weeks' notice, or until the sixth of July, whichever should come first.''

Jake felt a twinge of unease. "Why didn't the agency simply call me about this mix-up?"

He wasn't sure, but he thought she blushed ever so slightly.

"I insisted upon seeing you tonight."

"They still could have called."

"I wished to talk to you about this, alone, before bringing the agency into this."

"So they gave you my address? Just like that?"

She shifted. "Well, no. I also... told them that I needed to see you about Caleb's medication."

"He doesn't have any. He's as healthy as a horse."

She shrugged, her manner becoming stern again. "So I lied. I was a little desperate at the time."

"What do you want, Ms. McBride?" Jake demanded bluntly. Didn't she know that he didn't want to have anything to do with her? That he was the last person he wanted her to come to for help?

"I want to know why you left him with me so abruptly."

"I told you. I thought you knew he was coming."

"But once you learned I had no knowledge of such events, you could have stayed."

"I was late for work."

She sighed, eyeing him quite doubtfully. Frankly, he couldn't blame her. With him dressed as he was, she'd probably concluded that he'd spent the past few hours at the gym—but he didn't intend to explain himself. Jake had several lines of work that demanded his attention, and although his varied means of employment might be a little unorthodox to some, he really didn't care. He'd learned long ago that he was happiest when he challenged the norm.

"Mr. Turk."

"Jake."

"Jake. It seems to me that you've already formed some sort of... antagonism toward me."

"It's nothing personal."

"It *is* personal." She marched down the steps. "We met for the first time today, yet you treat me as if I'm some sort of... of... criminal. Forgive me if I take that personally!"

"I've already said everything that I need to say." With one last glance at the toddler, he said, "Take good care of Caleb for the next few weeks."

He tried to brush past her, but she grasped his forearm, stopping him. He glanced down at the point of contact, surprised by the nerve she'd displayed with such an action.

"I think you owe me an explanation. I think I have a right to know how all this happened, why you aren't still serving as his nanny, why you feel so... angry toward me." She used her free hand to sweep a lock of hair off her forehead. The dark strands were still pulled back in the coil she'd worn earlier, but some of the silky tresses were abandoning their hold, making her appear a little mussed—as well as a great deal more appealing. "And what is all this business about a two-month deadline?"

"Marlene wanted to make sure the boy would be happy with you."

"Well, he isn't."

"He just met you—and under rather unusual circumstances."

"What happens if I prove 'unfit'?"

Jake hesitated, wondering if he should admit the truth, that the boy would be brought to him, then decided that any such comment would merely open a can of worms he wasn't ready to deal with at the present time. So he said instead, "He'll be taken somewhere else—a sort of foster care."

"I see."

When Jake refused to speak, she seemed to draw inside herself for calm. That was one thing Jake had already learned about her. That this woman was most upset when the serene mask of control she wore strengthened into a mask of stone—as if she didn't want anyone, *anyone,* to glimpse her true emotions. But that blatant control had slipped after a few hours with a screaming toddler. He could see her pique, her irritation, her anger. For some reason, he found those emotions highly intriguing—even amusing.

She must have sensed a portion of his humor. "Look, could we just talk about this?" she blurted out.

"Why?"

"Please?"

"What about Caleb?"

"He's sleeping quite heavily. I doubt he'll interrupt us."

Jake tore his eyes away from the angry color that had appeared in her cheeks. That was what she'd been missing earlier that day. Color. It made her appear more feminine, less like a block of marble.

Nodding, he headed toward the porch. "Come on in."

"I'd rather go somewhere on neutral territory, if you don't mind."

"Fine. But I've got to shower and wash off the oil first."

He saw the way she eyed the sheen on his chest, then looked down at her hand, which had been coated with the slippery substance. She rubbed her fingers together as if she couldn't believe the evidence.

"Very well."

Jake used his keys to open the front door, then stood on the threshold, propping the screen open. "Do you want to wait inside or out?"

"In."

"Great."

When he didn't move, she finally squeezed past him, taking great care not to touch his chest.

His lips twitched in amusement—he couldn't help it. Allowing the screen to bang shut, he walked to Caleb, scooped him against his chest and carried him inside, laying him on the couch. The little boy grunted, rolling onto his side, then fell asleep again.

Jacob looked up to find McBride watching him in amazement.

"How did you do that?"

"Do what?"

"Every time I touch him, he wakes up and screams. You don't know all I had to do to get him to sleep in that swing out there!"

Jake only grinned. "I'll be right out."

He was halfway down the hall when she asked, "How long will you be?"

The expression she wore made it plain that she was less than comfortable with the whole situation—the baby, Jake's house. The way his body gleamed with oil. If not for the issue at hand, Jake might have enjoyed baiting her.

"Fifteen, twenty minutes."

"Fine."

He paused, irritated by the way this woman seemed determined to have the last word. As if he were already in her employ and needed her permission to shower.

But when he eyed her sternly, she was oblivious of his pique. The good manners his mother had instilled in him before she died demanded he ask, "Would you like something? A cola, beer?"

"No. Thank you."

Jake gestured toward the living room behind her. "Make yourself at home." There. At long last, he'd had the final word.

As he turned away, he flipped on the overhead light, then pulled his tank top over his head. A small gasp caused gooseflesh to prickle his shoulders.

"What happened to you?"

He twisted to look at his back in the mirror hanging across the room. The spot where he'd been hit with the sword was already beginning to turn a motley assortment of colors.

"Nothing more that an average pain-in-the-butt day, Ms. McBride," he responded, but the moment he dropped his arms, he saw the way Delaney stared—hard—at the taut expanse. Although Jake was not unfamiliar with such looks, and indeed often made his living from indulging such ideas, something about her careful scrutiny was disturbing. Perhaps it was because *she* was obviously so unsettled.

Delaney turned and walked away, obviously wanting it to look as if she were just trying to absorb her surroundings. But Jake could tell by the energy that began to crackle in the air around them that she didn't see the faded sofa and the other simple furnishings. He knew his assumption was correct when she glanced at him over her shoulder. Her gaze clung to the breadth of his chest, then slipped down to his hips before bouncing back up again. The flush staining her cheeks grew brighter.

"What do you *really* want, Ms. McBride?"

"I told you. I need some answers."

Her words managed to help him drag his eyes to a proper perspective, away from her bright eyes, her slim form, her cool beauty. "What makes you think I can give them to you?"

"You're the only one in this situation with any sort of inside knowledge of how this whole...*debacle* occurred. At the very least, you can tell me why Marlie chose *me* to take care of her son."

"She said you were kind."

"What?" The word was little more than a breath.

"She said you were kind. One of the kindest people she'd ever known."

"But...but I hardly knew her!"

He shrugged. "I guess the fact that you listened to her when she thought about giving Caleb up for adoption made her feel as if you were somehow special."

"What about the baby's father? What does he have to say about all this?"

"Marlene was never sure who Caleb's father was."

"Oh." She was clearly embarrassed by her lack of knowledge. "I didn't know." She turned to the bookcases, idly running her finger over the titles, but he knew she wasn't reading them. "How old is Caleb?"

"Sixteen months."

"Has it really been that long since he was born?"

It was a rhetorical question, but he answered all the same. "Yes."

She rubbed her brow, shaking her head. "Well, you would know." Turning to face him again, she leaned her shoulders against the shelves. "How long did you work for Marlie?"

"Sixteen months."

The answer was telling, and he knew in an instant that she caught its significance.

"Why?" she suddenly exclaimed. "Why would Marlie do this? Why wouldn't she just leave the boy with you?"

Jake knew he should tell her. He knew he should spell out the rest of the bargain. But he couldn't do it. Not when there was a chance, a slim chance, that Caleb might be better off with her. It all boiled down to that. What was best for Caleb. Even if it meant Jacob might lose him.

He couldn't prevent the tightness in his voice when he said, "You would have to ask her that."

"Yes. Of course."

He waited to see if she would ask any other questions, then said, "I'm going to shower."

He didn't know whether she responded. He shut the bathroom door behind him before she had time to open her mouth.

His retreat had been a necessity. For a moment, the businesslike facade of the woman who stood in his living room had melted, to reveal someone vulnerable, capable of infinite gentleness, someone who

might even be . . . kissable. And that was one part of
her personality he couldn't afford to explore.

DELANEY TOOK a steadying breath. Her plan to
confront Jake Turk wasn't working out quite as she'd
hoped. She'd come prepared to take the offensive,
but Jacob had disarmed her before she even began.

When she saw his Jeep pull into the driveway,
she'd been filled with a willful sense of purpose.
She'd meant to get the answers to her questions, as
well as a commitment from Jake to continue as Caleb's nanny. What she hadn't been prepared for was
the sight of so much . . . so much *flesh*. The man had
stepped from his car wearing little more than a rag-
ged scrap of a shirt and a pair of shorts cut from an
old pair of sweatpants. As he walked toward her, the
combination of sunset and shadows had played upon
his skin, underscoring the sculptured beauty of his
physique. Not until later had she discovered the effect was caused by baby oil slathered all over his
body.

Baby oil. There was something...unsettling about
a man who covered himself in baby oil—for heaven
only knew what reason. When she grasped his arm,
the muscles had been **h**ard and warm. Slick.

Disturbed by the wayward path of her own
thoughts, Delaney crossed to the couch, staring down
at the little boy who had unwittingly caused so much
confusion.

So innocent. So adorable. With his thatch of blond hair and his chubby cheeks, he would be a natural for commercials. He had a healthy, all-American wholesomeness that would inspire confidence in innumerable products.

Did she want to keep him? *Did* she want to complicate her life with the addition of a child?

Unlike most women her age, she had never been filled with panic by the ticking of her biological clock. She might be on the doorstep of thirty, but in her line of work she'd seen mothers have their first babies at forty, even fifty. She'd always felt that when the time was right, she would instinctively know.

Now that choice was being taken from her. If—as her lawyer and everyone else assured her was true—this boy was her responsibility for a few weeks, she would have to seriously consider keeping him. When she thought of sending him off to foster care, she wasn't sure she could do it. It wouldn't be fair to Caleb—or even the well-meaning Marlie.

But, heavens above, she didn't know how to care for a baby! She needed help. She needed . . .

A nanny.

Her lips firmed with renewed determination, and she slowly turned to stare at the bathroom door that separated her from Jacob Turk.

Surely he would agree. He'd seemed upset by the fact that Marlie hadn't given the boy to him. He was genuinely fond of the boy. She hoped he would *want* to resume his position—even though, for some reason, he didn't like *her*. She'd just have to change that opinion. Tonight.

When she heard the water cease, Delaney was well prepared for what she felt would be the ensuing battle. But her courage nearly deserted her when Jake emerged from the steamy bathroom. Except for a pair of half-buttoned jeans, he was as bare as the day he'd been born. Strong feet led to muscled calves and thighs encased in worn denim. A patch of color peeked above the placket of his jeans, proclaiming the existence of a scant pair of briefs. Then there was nothing but skin as far as the eye could see. Water dappled the lean contours of his stomach and the musculature of his chest. His shoulders were wide and well-defined.

His arms flexed and contracted as he rubbed a towel over his hair. After stretching like a well-fed cat, Jake tossed the towel into the bathroom and raked a comb through the strands, which reached midway down his back. "I'll be ready in a minute."

Before she could lose her presence of mind yet another time, Delaney took the proverbial bull by the horns and asked, "When will you be resuming your position as Caleb's nanny?"

Jake's hand dropped, but he didn't speak. He stood with his feet braced apart, his arms held loosely to his sides. Despite his relaxed stance, he gave the impression of being ready for the confrontation.

"I won't be coming back."

The blunt refusal surprised her more than it should have.

"Why not?" she demanded.

"I've got my reasons."

"I think I should hear them."

He didn't bother to reply. He merely turned and strode down the hall. When he disappeared through the far door, she followed, barely registering the fact that she'd stormed uninvited into a strange man's bedroom.

"After all that's happened today, all that I've gone through to track you down—just to talk to you!—I think you could have the courtesy to offer a few simple explanations."

"I don't owe you anything." He took a T-shirt from his dresser and tugged it over his head. "I worked for Marlene Detry, not for you."

"What does that matter? Caleb still needs you. Why won't you even *consider* working with me?" She gestured vaguely toward the other room. "If I'd been given some warning that this was going to happen, I could have been...prepared in some way. But to drop the child in my lap and expect me to cope..." When he made no comment, she demanded, "Why?"

"You couldn't afford me, for one thing. I'm very expensive."

She blinked at him in astonishment. It was the last argument she would have expected from a man who looked anything but worldly.

"I think I could make the necessary payments. Is that your only concern? The money?"

He didn't answer. He merely looked at her, his eyes dark and hooded.

"Caleb would be confused about how to interact with you if I returned."

"He's been given a new mother, a new home. Wouldn't one familiar face amid all those changes prove to be a comfort?"

He didn't answer.

"Well?" she asked.

"There are other reasons."

"What? What could possibly cause you to have such second thoughts?"

Before she knew what he meant to do, Jake snagged her wrist and jerked her forward. Clasping her chin, he forced her to turn and study her reflection in the full-length mirror attached to his closet door. "That's one reason."

"I don't underst—"

"I've got a reputation, my own code of ethics, a set of professional values. I've worked hard at what I do, and I've made a name for myself—but only because I've adhered to one simple rule. I don't take a job from a tempting lady. Someday I might decide to return to this line of work, and I won't let you ruin that for me."

"Ruin it? *Ruin* it?" She tried to struggle free, but he held her in a manaclelike grip. "How am I supposed to do that, when all I'm asking is that you serve as Caleb's nanny?"

Something within Jake snapped. The frustration of the day, combined with his uncharacteristic reactions to this woman, bubbled up inside him. "Dammit, woman. Can you possibly be that dense?" He twisted her in his arms, then yanked her tightly against the wall of his body.

Delaney was immediately conscious of the damp heat of his flesh and the bulge of each leanly honed muscle. He smelled of soap and water and man. They stood locked together—thigh to thigh, hip to hip.

Jake grew still. Completely and utterly still. When he spoke, his voice was husky and whiskey-smooth. "I've seen through you, McBride. From the very beginning, you've tried to impress me with those icy stares and cool comments, but I've caught a peek at what's hidden underneath, and it can cause nothing but trouble. For both of us. There are definite reasons why we mustn't get to know each other on anything but the level of acquaintances."

She caught her breath in a gasping manner that made him focus on her lips. When she didn't keep them pressed so tightly together, they were quite full, quite lovely. The fact merely strengthened his convictions. It would be wrong to get to know this woman, to spend time with her on a day-to-day basis. It would make a complicated situation even more difficult.

But even as the thoughts raced through his head, he couldn't help holding her a little longer, staring at her, memorizing the face of the person who might become Caleb's future mother.

"Why do you hide it, McBride? Surely you must know what runs through a man's head every time he looks at someone like you?" There was a thread of surprise in his tone, as if he hadn't meant to admit such a thing to himself, let alone to her. "That hair, that suit, that don't-touch-me-or-I'll-slap-you demeanor."

Again she gasped, struggling to free herself. "I don't think that this has anything to do with the matter under discussion."

Jake stared at her with something akin to amazement. "You really don't get it, do you?" He shifted her in his arms, splaying broad hands over her shoulders. "I'm a man who has built a career for himself by involving myself with the children. Only the children. I don't associate with the parents, I never have. I keep such relationships strictly professional. You, on the other hand, would prove to be a distinct complication. A distraction."

"Only if you make me one."

He knew the moment she uttered the words that she wished she could take them back. The room shuddered with a silken heat.

"How could I resist?" Jake murmured, just before he bent his head and closed his mouth over hers. It was a tentative exploration. Touching, testing, quenching the need he'd felt to do just that ever since the moment he'd seen her standing on his porch, her hair a little askew, her expression a bit bewildered.

"No," Delaney managed to whisper, twisting her head away.

He forced her to look at him. His expression caused the air to lock in her body as his features settled into fierce, nearly primitive lines. Then his hands gentled. He wove his fingers into the strands of her hair, as if savoring the weight, the texture, and then he bent for another kiss.

This time, he tasted her, courted her, wooed her. His tongue asked for entry to her lips and she whimpered deep in her throat. When he lifted his head, his mouth hovered so close that his breath became hers. His eyes flashed with indecision even as his hips nudged closer.

Delaney's palms cupped his waist—though how they'd come to rest there, she didn't know. She sensed the struggle mounting in him—both physically and emotionally. But it could never compare to the tempest he'd inspired inside her. She couldn't think, couldn't move. How could he unsettle her so completely in such a short space of time?

Evidently Jake was asking himself the same questions, because he dropped his hands to his sides. After taking one deep, calming breath, he swore and walked from the room. By the time Delaney gathered her wits enough to follow him, he'd tucked his shirt into his jeans and fastened the snap.

Delaney watched him for a moment in indecision, and then her gaze bounced to the boy. "Perhaps it *would* be better if I go. I'll call the placement agencies and put myself on their lists and..." Unable to finish the statement, knowing that it could be months before she had any kind of help, she walked to the couch. Awkwardly she surveyed Caleb, considering how best to lift him.

Sighing, Jake pushed her aside.

Delaney forced herself to swallow her pride. "Please. Couldn't you help us—just temporarily?"

"No."

She fought the urge to stamp her foot at his blatant stubbornness. "Why not?"

He caught her face, forcing her to look at him, so that she had no doubt he meant to frighten her away by the disturbing physical chemistry that flared between them. "Because I didn't want to be Caleb's nanny. I wanted to be his guardian—but the job was given to you for a few weeks, and I won't go against his mother's wishes. Added to that is the fact that I find you intriguing—even attractive."

She huffed at that backhanded compliment, but he continued without pause. "Those emotions don't mix with becoming the live-in help."

Live-in help...

Why hadn't it occurred to her that Jake's position as a nanny would mean living with the child? Living with *her?*

"So we finally understand each other," he murmured.

She nodded, but when she would have reached for the boy, he pushed her aside, lifting Caleb into his arms.

Silently, they made their way to a Jaguar parked at the curb. Pleased that she'd at least fitted the passenger side with a child's safety seat, Jake quickly strapped him in, then closed the door, all without waking the boy.

Delaney stood before him, so serious, so proud. Her hair gleamed in the dim light, falling loose from its pins. Jake was amazed by the way a simple kiss had eased the iron from her stance, making her appear quite...beautiful. Even if he were desperate for a job, she'd be the last thing he needed in an employer. She would be dangerous. She would distract him to no end and tempt him to stray from his duties.

When Jake didn't speak, she obviously took his prolonged silence for a dismissal. Holding herself erect and proud, she rounded the car. Once at the driver's side, she paused. He could feel her watching him. The sultry night air crowded close. A thousand chips of starlight whispered in the quiet.

At that moment, Jake realized that she really meant to go. She would not approach him again.

It was for the best, he told himself. He didn't really have time to involve himself in anything but business at this point. His mental and physical energies were already stretched to the limit.

"Goodbye, Mr. Turk," she said, slipping into the car.

He opened his mouth to say something more, but closed it again. It was better this way, he told himself again. Much better.

Chapter Four

The sun was hot against his face as Jake brought his vintage Harley to a stop in front of Marlene Detry's town house. The moving van he and his brother had rented rolled to a halt at the curb. Waving to Nick to follow, Jake made his way to the house and let himself in.

"We'll only take Caleb's things," he said, pointing to a room at the far end of the hall.

Nick headed in that direction, leaving Jake alone in the hall. For several long moments, he remained where he was, absorbing the silence.

The house had never been this still in the sixteen months he lived here. There'd been a child here. A little boy who seemed to infuse the home with his energy. Now that he was gone, with no hope of his ever coming back here, the place was more lifeless than seemed possible.

"Where are we going to take this stuff?" Nick asked as he passed Jake in the hall, carrying a sturdy oak rocker.

"I'll keep it in the moving van for now," Jake said, not about to admit to Nick that only the night before he'd had an argument with Caleb's new guardian. At the time, he hadn't stopped to think that, after burning his bridges, he would be forced to cross them again—and so soon. He'd forgotten that he had no idea where Delaney McBride lived and that he would have to arrange for the delivery of Caleb's things.

"Hey, are you going to give me a hand or not?" Nick demanded, playfully punching him in the ribs as he made his way back into the house.

"Yeah. I'll be right there."

But it was harder than he'd thought it would be to step into the nursery—a nursery he had decorated, because Marlene was too busy. He studied the walls, with their hand-painted murals: a football stadium filled with crowds of onlookers, the sunny, cloud-studded sky of the ceiling, the football-shaped light fixture, the yard-marked floor and the carved end zones on either side.

With each minute that passed, a tension began to fill his body, causing his hands to curl into fists and his jaw to tense.

Nick looked up.

"What's the matter?"

Jake would have remained silent, kept his thoughts to himself, but Nick was his brother—probably the only man who would understand.

"I met the woman who could be Caleb's new guardian."

"Oh?"

"She doesn't have a clue what to do with the boy."

Nick grinned. "Then she'll be eliminated as a choice for guardianship."

Jake didn't immediately answer.

"Won't she?"

"She strikes me as the type who could be a fast learner. She's also very...gentle."

"That might sway the lawyer a bit now, but how will gentleness help her when Caleb's sixteen? I'm sure that will be taken into consideration."

"Maybe." Jake hesitated before saying, "She came to see me again last night."

Just as he had anticipated, Nick grew still, displaying without a word that he was listening intently.

"It seems there's some glitch in the contract. Marlene didn't cancel it."

"So what?"

"So—" he sighed "—I am obligated to continue caring for Caleb for another six weeks."

One of Nick's brows raised, and Jake knew he was thinking of all the things that Jake had left unsaid. The fact that he'd been given the perfect opportunity to be with Caleb during the trial period, to see how McBride handled the situation, to test Caleb's reactions himself. But also unspoken was the fact that if Caleb was given to Delaney McBride, the goodbyes wouldn't be any easier in six weeks.

"Other than being gentle, what's the woman like?"

"Stuffy. Uptight."

But that wasn't really true. He suspected that the woman he'd encountered the day before would behave far differently if a man had the time to get to know her. To see what was hidden beneath that severe hairdo and those guarded eyes. It might even prove to be a challenge.

"What are you going to do?"

Jake took a deep breath, propping his hands on his hips and surveying the room where he'd spent so much time during the past sixteen months.

"I don't know."

But they both saw through the lie.

Before the day was out, Jake would be resuming his role as Caleb's nanny.

Even if he had to make Ms. McBride think she was the one responsible for his change of heart.

"No, Caleb, please. Please, don't cry!"

The baby wasn't listening. Or he didn't understand. Or he was punishing her. Whatever the reason, he continued to sob, fat tears rolling down his cheeks, his fists rubbing at his eyes.

Delaney jiggled him as much as she could while she surveyed the shattered glass and debris still scattered over the laboratory floor.

Caleb hated her. She was sure he did. It was obvious that he didn't understand the change in his lifestyle and he blamed her for the heartache. He didn't want to be held. He didn't want to be left alone. He didn't want food or sleep or clean diapers. And whatever he *did* want, she hadn't discovered it yet.

Burt Addleman, her assistant, fought back a chuckle, ducking his head.

"I saw that smirk, Burt."

He laughed openly. "You should see your face, Delaney. I don't know whose scowl is fiercer—yours or his."

"Thanks for the compliment."

"Anytime."

Burt had been supervising the janitorial staff for nearly an hour as they cleaned up the mess made the day before, when Willie Parker had thrown vials, specimen jars and blood samples all over the floor and walls. Unfortunately, most of the debris had been given a day to set in and dry, since it had taken until this afternoon for the police to give them permission to enter the room.

"Why don't you take him to day-care?"

"I tried that," Delaney said. "He went into hysterics. You would have thought I was leading him to the gas chamber."

"I suppose, what with all the changes he's suffered, he's just a little confused."

"That may be true." She bounced the boy, patting his back. "But if he doesn't stop throwing tantrums like this, we're both going to need sedation."

"Kids," Burt said fondly, shaking his head. He was the father of six teenage girls. "You can't live with 'em—" he held up a sealed test tube, his eyes growing sad "—you can't stand living without 'em."

Delaney felt her heart wrench a little as she watched Burt examine the cracked tube, which had once held a frozen fertilized egg belonging to a couple in Reno, Nevada, who had been trying for over fifteen years to have a child.

"I hope they hang the creep," he muttered to himself, tossing it into the waste receptacle with all the other ruined samples.

"Not a chance." When Burt looked at her, Delaney shrugged. "The board, despite my protestations, voted against pressing charges. Said they 'didn't care to incur any adverse publicity.'" She quoted them succinctly. "Willie Parker walked just after noon."

Burt's lips tightened, and he stood, smoothing a hand over his balding pate. "Well, in my opinion, they should have walked him right over here to help clean up this mess. Maybe then it would have sunk into his thick skull just what he destroyed in trying to obtain sperm samples that were accidentally destroyed in a lab fire more than five years ago."

Delaney couldn't have agreed more. So much work—not just for them, but for their clients. It would take months to recover from a single day of havoc.

"Here," Burt said, extending his arms. "Let me hold the squirt for a minute."

The moment he took the boy, Caleb's cries eased. He stared at Burt, wide-eyed, then patted the man's cheek with a chubby fist.

"Well, what do you know? He likes me."

"Don't take it personally," Delaney retorted, flexing her arms to ease stiff muscles. "He's a first-class chauvinist. He just hates women."

"Dr. McBride?"

Delaney looked up to find Linda waving at her from the doorway. Lifting one brow queryingly, Delaney waited for the other woman to come into the room. Instead, Linda motioned for Delaney to meet her in the hall.

She hesitated, but Burt waved her away. "Go on. I'll take care of him for a minute or two."

"Thanks, Burt."

Slipping her hands into the pockets of her lab coat, Delaney moved into the hall. To her amusement, she found Linda waiting for her well away from the door and the curious ears of the other lab workers.

"Yes?"

Linda glanced furtively over her shoulder, as if she were some sort of spy in a B-grade movie. Then she took Delaney's portable phone from the pocket of her jacket. "I was closing up the reception area when your briefcase started ringing. Geez, I wish you'd get a private line put into the office. I hate it when I have to answer your luggage."

"So you brought the phone all the way here to inform me that my mother wanted to talk to me?" Very few people had the number to her mobile phone. She couldn't think of one who would necessitate a clandestine meeting in the passageway.

"It wasn't your mother. It was Jake Turk."

"Jake?" She tried to deny the way her heart made a little jump. "Jake *Turk?*"

"Yes. Isn't he the one who brought Caleb? The man who came to the office yesterday?"

Delaney nodded. Along with supervising the cleanup of the lab room, she'd spent most of the morning looking for someone who could help her with Caleb. Apart from an excited promise from her mother to come see the boy sometime this week, she'd had no luck. Her mother had put a further crimp in things by saying she would wait as long as possible before visiting, in order to give Delaney and Caleb time to "bond."

So far, the only real "bonding" to occur had been by the breakfast cereal Caleb had thrown on the floor that morning.

"Do you want to talk to Mr. Turk?"

Delaney almost snatched the phone from her hand. She prayed that he'd changed his mind, regretted everything he'd said and was hoping to come back as Caleb's nanny.

"Did he say what he wanted?"

"No. He asked that you get in touch with him at work. He tried to get you at home, and no one answered. He said the nanny agency was kind enough to give him this number." When Delaney stood rooted to the spot, Linda demanded, "Well, what are you waiting for? Call the man! Now! You can't leave anyone who looks like that dangling for long!"

"This isn't an assignation, Linda."

"No... but it could be. Call him quick!"

Chuckling, Delaney glanced at the phone message Linda had handed her and punched the appropriate sequence of numbers. She held the receiver to her ear and waited for someone to answer. Linda never failed to lift her spirits. Her secretary's wide grin, gamine features and bright red hair had endeared her to Delaney the second the older woman walked into the job interview three years before. Delaney had hired her on the spot, and had never regretted the impulse.

"Well?" Linda asked when Delaney's brow creased.

"No one is answering. Are you sure this is the right number?"

"Positive."

The phone rang nearly a half-dozen more times before someone answered. "Yeah!"

"Jacob Turk, please."

"Is that you, McBride?"

She ignored Linda, knowing that her friend wouldn't budge an inch, for fear of missing some tidbit of the conversation.

"Yes. This is—"

"Look, I forgot that I'd agreed to help you move the crib and the high chair. So I guess our paths are about to cross again, no matter how much either of us might regret it."

Delaney strained to hear him through the giggling and music she could hear in the background. It sounded as if a noisy party were in progress, and Delaney felt a shred of suspicion, then a rush of disappointment.

"I see."

"No. No, you don't see," he said, interrupting her. From the other end of the line, Delaney heard a thump and a burst of drums and guitars, and then Jake came back on the line. "McBride? Are you still there?"

"Yes."

"Look, I've only got a few hours free this evening. If you want to meet me at my job, I'll show you what I've gathered already. I've loaded his furniture and clothes into a van, but you'll want to check Marlene's place and make sure there's nothing else you need. Otherwise, the stuff will probably be confiscated. Can you meet me tonight or not?"

"I've got plans with a friend...." Linda was still watching Delaney with avid eyes. Linda had told

Delaney she'd take her somewhere for a birthday dinner, but Delaney was sure she'd understand if there was a change of plans.

Linda must have heard part of Jake's request, because she whispered, "Go. Go!"

"Yes, I'm free."

"Good. Would you mind meeting me here at Twin Towers? I've got a break coming up in about an hour. We can check out the van in between my shifts. I'll be done at seven, and then we'll go to Marlene's."

"Fine."

"You don't mind coming here?" Despite the heavy throb of drums, she heard the surprise in his voice.

"No, I don't mind."

"Got a pen? I've only got a minute to give you directions."

"Yes, I've got a pen." However, she didn't have a thing to write on except her sleeve. Seeing her predicament, Linda raced into the lab, tore a sheet of paper from one of the computer printers and ran back.

Caleb, attracted by the woman's frantic movements, struggled to get down from Burt's arms. As soon as his feet hit the floor, he was running toward the door.

Knowing she had only a minute before the baby escaped into the hall and ran who knew where, Delaney dashed to grasp the straps of his overalls. Since Delaney couldn't juggle baby, phone, pen and paper, Linda snatched the pen from Delaney's hand. As Jake gave her the directions, she repeated the gist of them to Linda, who transcribed them in a rushed, scrawling hand.

"Drive to Twin Towers. Ask the parking officials to direct me to Safety and Security. Gordie will meet me and Caleb there and take us to you." The way he underscored the fact that Caleb was to be present did not escape her attention.

"Got it?"

"Yes, but—"

"Gotta go. See you in a few."

In a few what? The line disconnected before she could find out.

"Who's Gordie?"

Delaney absently disconnected the phone and shrugged. Caleb grunted, pulling against her grip, but she held firm.

"Where does this guy—Jake—work?"

"Well, he was a full-time nanny, but now it seems he's with the Twin Towers theme park."

Linda's brows rose. "As what?"

"I haven't the faintest idea. He must be a ride attendant or something." When Caleb began to sink to the floor, in the beginnings of another tantrum, she scooped him onto her hip and handed him the phone to amuse him.

"The man is over thirty years old and took a job that makes minimum wage at an amusement park?" The excitement faded from Linda's features, to be replaced with an obvious regret. "Damn. I was hoping this was someone who could drag you into a meaningful relationship. Instead, he's just a jock with no ambition." Offering a loud sigh of commiseration, she retreated in the direction of Delaney's offices.

Linda's words rang in her head for a moment, but Delaney pushed her reaction away, absently jiggling the baby on her hip as he attempted to devour one end of the phone. Jake wasn't a "jock with no ambition." There was more to him than that. She sensed it—*knew* it somehow.

Turning, she retraced her steps to the lab. When Caleb realized that they were going to return to where they'd been and were not going "out" or "away" or "bye-bye", his eyes widened like those of a trapped rabbit ready to bolt. Then he opened his mouth, screwed his eyes shut, and began to scream.

Delaney pressed her lips together in a firm line to keep from groaning aloud.

Mr. Jacob Turk would have to come back as the boy's nanny. It was the only logical solution to this mess.

And she would see to it tonight that he agreed.

WITHIN THIRTY MINUTES, Delaney and Caleb passed through the arched, multilaned entrance to the Twin Towers theme park. Delaney felt a twinge of anxiety as the parking attendant slipped an orange Staff marker beneath the windshield wiper of her car, knowing that her showdown with Jacob Turk was now inevitable.

The attendant pointed to a mechanical gate nearly hidden behind a tangled clematis vine. "I've already called ahead, and someone will be there to meet you, Ms. McBride. You can use any of the parking spaces on the east side of the lot."

"Thank you." Scrolling her window back into place, Delaney eased into the appropriate lane. Just as her car neared the gate, the metal portal rolled to the side, allowing her to enter the cramped employee parking lot.

There were none of the elaborate amenities present in the public portion of the complex. This area gave a different perspective on those who worked here. Simple clapboard buildings framed the asphalt square. There were no signs or directions, as if it were simply assumed that anyone who entered would know where to go.

Delaney maneuvered the car into a narrow parking place, then, unhooking Caleb from his seat, hefted him onto her hip. Maybe this was another sort of bonding, she concluded wryly, considering the fact that they seemed permanently attached at that spot.

Caleb immediately began to work his way into a hiccuping set of near-sobs. She couldn't blame him, really. He looked as hot and tired and rumpled as she did. And since she was not on his list of favorite people, she supposed his attitude was to be expected. Even so, it hurt to think that he disliked her so much. She would have done anything at this point to see him smile, to hear him laugh. To know that he wasn't as tortured as he appeared.

"Nice set of wheels."

She whirled to find a lanky, bizarrely dressed man watching her from where he lay upon the battered hood of a vintage Mustang convertible. Judging by his relaxed pose and the way he regarded her beneath lazy, half-closed eyelids, he'd been trying to improve his tan.

"Late-model Jaguar, V12 engine. Quite a showpiece."

"Really?" She gazed at the vehicle in disbelief. It had been a gift from her father after she earned her third Ph.D. As an only child, she tended to be spoiled by her parents with expensive gifts and outrageous offers of vacations. As far as the Jaguar was concerned, the gesture had been a bit wasted. She wasn't really a car person. As long as the vehicle she used had four wheels, a radio and some sort of air-conditioning, she'd drive just about anything.

"You Delaney McBride?"

"Yes. I am."

He sighed and rose to a sitting position with a molasses-in-winter grace, then eased from the car with excruciating slowness. Delaney had plenty of time to absorb the man's bright red high-tops, baggy pleated pants, green polka-dot suspenders and sleeveless orange T-shirt. His wavy dust brown hair exploded in tousled wisps from a severely receding hairline.

"Gordie."

"Beg pardon?"

"I'm Gordie." He chucked Caleb under the chin, and the boy immediately giggled and held out his arms to be taken. It was obvious that Gordie was a familiar face to Caleb, and that the boy would much rather spend time with him. Delaney couldn't quite account for the twinge of failure she experienced at such a thought—as well as at the fact that it had taken someone else to make him laugh the way she'd wanted to make him do.

With the barest nudge of his shoulder, Gordie motioned for Delaney to follow him. "This way."

Delaney caught up to him quickly enough, then had to adjust her stride to his getting-nowhere-fast amble.

"Jacob told me you would take me to him."

"Jacob?" Gordie's lips cracked in a grin.

"Jacob Turk."

The grin didn't ease.

"You are taking me to him, aren't you?"

"Yep." The word was rich with private laughter. "Jacob will be at the box."

"Box?"

"Sandbox."

Gordie's cryptic explanation didn't give her the slightest clue to what he meant. Deciding that he must not be much of a talker, she followed him to a low, squat building in the center of the complex.

Shifting Caleb to one hip, Gordie held open a battered screen door and motioned for her to proceed him into a long, tunnellike hall lit by a dozen bare bulbs suspended from the ceiling.

"Where are we?" she asked as he led her through a mouse's maze of corridors.

"Safety and Security is above us. We go below." With a sweep of his hand, he gestured toward an old freight elevator. "This is quicker than the stairs."

Deciding she would never find her way back alone, Delaney stepped into the car. The metal doors rattled closed, and Gordie punched a warped button near the bottom of the panel. The plastic disk had long since lost any sign of a recognizable number.

The car stopped with a jolt, and the cage squeaked open, revealing a long dim tunnel.

"Looks like something out of a Hitchcock movie, doesn't it?" Gordie commented as he shuffled forward.

Delaney was beginning to wonder what in the world she was doing following this strange man several levels beneath the park. Just what kind of job did Jake Turk have? Did he stoke the boilers or work in some dreadful under-the-earth maintenance position?

"This way." Gordie held open a heavy metal door. "It hasn't started yet."

"Started?"

"The show."

Delaney still had no idea what he meant, but she followed him past three hulking pop machines to a metal spiral staircase.

"You may as well watch from the booth. It's the best seat in the house."

Deciding that her questions would have to wait until she could talk to someone who didn't speak in code, Delaney followed him up the stairs.

Caleb's head bobbed above Gordie's shoulder, and for the first time that she could remember, he studied her with something other than dislike. In fact, he eyed her curiously, obviously wondering how she fit in with all the changes that had been made in his usual routines.

He looked at Gordie again, then back at her, then held out a hand and waved, as if to say, "Bye-bye."

She pressed her lips together in determination. Oh, no. She was not going away so quickly, so easily. Marlie had trusted her to care for this child, and she would—and, by heaven, she would find a way to make him like her in the process.

Feeling a little like Scarlett O'Hara giving her "I will not go hungry again" speech, she marched up the rest of the steps. They had climbed at least the equivalent of three flights before she dared to ask, "Where are we, exactly?"

Gordie flashed her a look of surprise. "The pavilion. The tunnel led us under the main concourse of the park, right to the auditorium." He stopped at the summit of the stairs and held open another heavy metal door. "After you."

Relieved that they'd finally finished their ascent, Delaney stepped into the blackened room. Her first impression was that she'd entered a cockpit copied from *Star Wars*. The booth was little bigger than her hall closet at home, but it was filled with blinking computers, control panels, electronic equipment and—quite blissfully—enough arctic air-conditioning to make a penguin happy.

A balding, middle-aged man glanced up from his fierce scrutiny of a paper-filled clipboard. "Caleb, my boy! Have you come to help me?" When he caught sight of Delaney, he scrambled to his feet. "Oh! I beg your pardon."

"Mel, this is Ms. McBride."

"Well. Well! Pleased to meet you, ma'am." He shoved his hand in her direction and, when she clasped it, gave her a hearty handshake.

"Thank you, Mr...."

"Twickel. Mel Twickel. But everybody calls me Mel." He reached behind him to roll a battered drafting stool toward her. "Have a seat. We're about a minute to curtain."

Still unsure of what she was supposed to be seeing, Delaney placed her purse on the floor and settled on the high cushion.

Mel took charge of Caleb, and it soon became obvious that the boy had been in this same spot on numerous occasions. He seemed to know which glittering buttons he was allowed to touch and which he was not. Mel put a battered baseball hat with the park's logo on Caleb's head and handed him a plastic microphone to play with—one that Delaney assumed had been left here just for that purpose.

"Can you see the stage well enough, ma'am?" Mel asked.

Delaney peered through the wide picture windows, then nearly gaped in surprise. Below her, a huge auditorium sloped down toward an intricate stage adorned with gargoyles, craggy stones, and a glistening ice-green moat. A wall of cascading water formed a huge liquid curtain that effectively screened the rest of the stage from view.

"Ma'am?"

"Yes, I can see."

Mel grunted in approval and settled back into his chair. "I'm afraid we'll be ignoring you for a little while."

"Should I take Caleb?"

"Nah. He's an old hand at this. Aren't you, partner?"

Caleb squealed and tugged at the man's bow tie. To Delaney's surprise, she turned to see that Gordie had donned a set of headphones. His eyes sparkled with energy, and he chattered into the slender mike as if he'd been given a shot of adrenaline.

"If you're sure, Mr. Tw—"

"Mel." He turned then, Caleb held securely on his lap.

Gordie reached out to punch a series of computer keys. "House lights down two-thirds. Cue music. Five, four, three, two, one. Cue curtain."

Delaney watched in utter fascination as, bit by bit, the wall of water obscuring the stage parted in the middle and began to retreat, moving toward the wings and leaving a trail of cascading droplets. Then, Mel leaned forward, and, in a deep Lou Rawls voice, began to speak: "Welcome to *The Legend of Tar....*" With a flick of his wrist, he hit a button that released a prerecorded combination of soundtrack music and narration.

Delaney felt a quick surge of surprise, then a burst of incredulity. *The Legend of Tar?* Linda had brought some of her out-of-town relatives through Twin Towers little more than a month ago. For weeks, she'd talked of "the bare-butt review." How had she described the costuming? At least half the cast wore loincloths, and the other half weren't so modestly dressed?

Delaney's eyes widened, her mouth grew dry. Surely Jake didn't work... He couldn't possibly be...

"Cue the spot for Jake—and make it really pretty, Pabst, we've got a visitor in the booth," Gordie was saying. "Yeah, she's here. She's a looker, too. Tall, leggy, a hazel-eyed brunette. Yes, hazel. I know, I know. He's a goner."

Delaney barely had time to flush beneath the one-sided banter before a primeval rhythm began to pound from the speakers lining the arched ceiling of the auditorium. The music swelled, the lights dimmed. Fog rolled eerily onto the stage.

Then a single spotlight speared through the artificial mist to illuminate a figure poised on the precipice of a man-made cliff. The golden glow caressed the naked shape of his back, the strong crease of his spine, muscular thighs, firm calves. The loincloth he wore was nothing more than a minuscule scrap of fabric, offering no protection from her greedy eyes. She recognized the figure immediately, remembering the dark brown-black hair tumbling past his shoulders and the oil-coated bronze skin.

Jacob Turk.

The man was beautiful. Absolutely beautiful. More beautiful than any man had a right to be. Yet at one time he'd been Caleb's nanny. A *nanny?*

The rest of the show took place in a haze of unreality for Delaney. When the last light dimmed and the music reached a thundering crescendo, she had no idea what the plot line had been or how many other characters had been introduced onto the stage. She'd spent the entire time watching Jake Turk.

As Gordie rose from his chair and gestured for her to follow, she discovered her knees were shaky. Her heart pounded as if she'd just run up a flight of stairs—all from watching the blatant display of Jake's body. The show had been aimed toward the adolescent audience who read *The Legend of Tar* and avidly followed the cartoon characters each Saturday morning, but there had been plenty to attract adults to the display, as well. Especially female adults. The primitive beat of the music, combined with muscular men in loincloths swinging broadswords at one another had crossed the bounds of entertainment and become something purely sexual.

Now it was time to join the man in person.

Gordie took Caleb from Mel's lap, and she was glad. At this moment, she was afraid she might drop him.

"This way."

Once again, she followed Gordie into the bowels of the building. He stopped next to a discreet unmarked door and knocked once. "You decent?"

The door whipped open to display the broad, well-formed chest she'd been staring at all evening. When her gaze lifted, she found Jacob Turk regarding her with dark, piercing eyes. "Thanks, Gordo."

Tension crackled between them before Gordie could even manage to back away. He must have been aware of it, as well, because Gordie grinned. "My pleasure." He winked. "Enjoy yourselves now, y'hear?"

He handed Caleb to Delaney, who took him awkwardly. Delaney felt a betraying flush stain her cheeks as he disappeared down the hall. His throaty chuckles floated behind him, making the silence that followed somehow much more rich and intimate.

Jake was still breathing a little hard, and Delaney wasn't surprised. The forty-minute performance he'd given as Tar the Barbarian had been athletically demanding, allowing little or no opportunity for him to rest.

"Thanks for meeting me here."

"Sure."

The words they exchanged said nothing, but the way he was watching her spoke volumes—as if, somehow, he had divined how hard she was struggling to remain unaffected in his presence.

"Come on in." He held the door open, ushering her into a cramped dressing room that was little bigger than the booth upstairs. Two walls were lined with mirrors and makeup lights. Another wall held a battered couch and two wooden lockers.

"Thanks." She tried to keep as much space as possible between them as she crossed to set Caleb on one of the counters. She'd had no idea how tiring it could be to carry a toddler as much as she had the past two days.

"Yo, Jake!"

She jumped when the shout came from the far side of the space where another door led into what she assumed must be the shower room. A tall, ebony-skinned man wearing thigh-high boots and a toga-like leather jerkin stepped from behind the portal. Vaguely Delaney remembered the actor had served as the archvillain in the show. He came to a startled halt when he saw her.

"Doug Baker, this is Delaney McBride."

The other man nodded politely and shook her hand. "Nice to meet you. We've heard... all about you." His grin was as impudent and full of private amusement as Gordie's had been. "I'll just get out of your way."

Releasing her hand, he slapped Jake on the back, then disappeared.

This time, Delaney knew they were completely alone with Caleb. She could hear the distant drip-drip of a leaky shower head, and her own pounding heart. The cool air-conditioned draft that flowed from the vent over her head caressed her skin and brought with it the smell of baby oil and male musk.

Jake took a step forward, another, and another, crowding her, forcing her to shrink back to avoid brushing against his oiled body.

"So, Ms. McBride?" he murmured. "How has your first day of motherhood been?"

Chapter Five

"Awful. Just awful."

Delaney could have bitten her tongue in half when the truth burst free of its own volition. But Jake only grinned, gesturing toward the couch.

"Have a seat."

To get there, she would have to pass him in a much closer proximity than she would care to do. She could already sense the heat of his body, see the beads of perspiration on his brow and the rivulets coursing down the middle of his chest to that hard washboard stomach—

Stop it!

Her arms tightened around Caleb in reflex, and he grunted, pushing against her chest with both hands.

"Is something wrong?"

Jake's voice was like the low purr of a jungle cat, and just as disturbing. Alluring, but dangerous all the same. And with him dressed the way he was, the Tarzanlike metaphor was difficult to dismiss. For the first time in hours, she was glad to have a baby glued to her hip, glad for the barrier it provided against this man's physique.

"I hope you don't mind," Jake said, breaking into her thoughts.

Delaney had to wrench her eyes away from the brass studs that dotted his belt.

"But I don't think I'll change," he continued.

"Oh?" Dear heaven above, was she about to hold court with a man who wore nothing but a swatch of leather around his hips? Was she about to convince *him* that *she* was in charge?

Seeing no other alternative, she made her way around Jake's massive frame and sank onto the worn couch, hugging Caleb to her.

"Down!" He struggled against her grasp, groaning with the effort of trying to ease the tight band of her arms around his waist. But she didn't let him go. She couldn't.

"Normally, the cast keeps their costumes on and takes a dinner break at one of the surface restaurants about now—good PR and all that. I begged off eating at one of the more public restaurants, but since I won't have time to change afterward I thought I'd stay..."

He allowed the end of the sentence to trail away, as if the consequences were obvious. The only thing obvious to Delaney was that she had never seen a man so exposed. So virile. So... beautiful.

Jake took a towel from the counter and blotted at the sweat beading his face and chest. Delaney was almost afraid to see the moisture obliterated. It had given her something specific to focus upon so that she didn't have to absorb the entire man.

Caleb squealed, and not wanting him to begin a temper tantrum here, in front of his Nanny Jake, she set him on the floor beside her, holding tightly to the straps of his overalls. Swallowing against the dryness gathering in her throat, she hoped the little boy could form some sort of anchor for her wayward thoughts. Normally an organized person, a poised person, a reserved person, she couldn't account for the way her knees were suddenly trembling and her brain was refusing to function properly.

"Doug is arranging for some sandwiches and such to be sent to one of the picnic areas near here. Not exactly what Caleb is used to eating, but it will do in a pinch." He grabbed a towel from the stack on the makeup counter. "I'll just wipe off the oil first."

Delaney had to force herself to keep from staring. "I see."

Caleb squirmed in her grip, casting her a malevolent glance and clamoring for Jake to hold him. Forced to release him, Delaney watched as the boy ran forward to wrap his arms around Jake's knee. She clasped her hands together, trying to find something, anything, in the room, on the walls, that could hold her attention.

Anything but Jacob Turk.

Searching for some innocuous topic of conversation, she asked, "What *is* Caleb accustomed to eating?"

"I've always seen to it that he gets nutritional meals. Lots of vegetables, breads, cereals, a little meat."

She nodded as if she understood, but in reality, Delaney didn't have a clue as to how to feed a boy Caleb's age. Was she to choose his meals from those little jars of food at the grocery store, or did he eat like "real people"? So far, she'd been feeding him from the containers Jake had left in the diaper bag. Some kind of cold cereal, and a few nasty-looking crackers.

She shot a defensive look at Caleb, only to find him staring at her as if she were some evil stepmother. Had she been starving him? Was that why he was so distraught? That thought alone was able to instill her with more guilt than she would have thought humanly possible.

Jake disengaged himself from the boy's grasp and disappeared through the far door, tossing the towel into a hamper. Through it all, Caleb continued to stare at her with overt malevolence, leaving her feeling wretched and inadequate. The little boy was probably being tortured under her care. That must be why he cried so much.

"Ready?"

She started when Jake returned, sporting a tissue to wipe Caleb's nose with. Again she felt a stab of inadequacy. She should have been the one to get it. That way, Jake wouldn't have thought her a total fool.

"Yes, I suppose." She stood, smoothing down the line of her silk skirt, feeling suddenly overdressed and gawky. Despite all her degrees, all her schooling, she didn't know how to do something so simple as taking care of a child. And the fact that she must look like a fool in Jake's eyes made her lack of knowledge even more upsetting.

She trailed a few steps behind Jake and Caleb as they headed into the hall. Watching his every move, she tried to determine how he carried the child, what kinds of comments he made, how he played with him. But it was no use. The rapport between them was something that could not be easily duplicated.

Jake backtracked much of the tangled route Delaney had taken to get to him in the first place, until finally they emerged into the blast of the hot sun. Even Caleb flinched at the weather, wrapping his arms around Jake's neck and glaring over Jake's shoulder at Delaney. He still didn't know who she was or why she had come into his life. But there was more to his apparent anger than that. Hunger? Did he look hungry?

"This is the van with his things." Jake paused in front of an imposing yellow rental van and rolled the back door open, leaving Delaney to stare at the contents. From what she could see, there was a crib, a rocker, a dresser, mounds of stuffed animals and a few pictures. But what caught her attention was the vintage Harley motorcycle tucked against the side. It obviously didn't belong to Caleb. Just looking at it brought all sorts of images. Jake zooming down the street, his chest bare, his hair streaming behind him—

"Well?"

"That looks...fine."

Jake eyed her for several moments, obviously waiting for some other kind of reaction, but when none was forthcoming, he lowered the door and locked it. "Good." He turned to the boy. "How about something to eat?"

Caleb clapped his hands, causing Delaney's guilt to intensify. Lord, she was going to kill this child before she got the hang of caring for him.

They made their way back through the park, Jake leading them down several paths that she was sure the public had never seen before, until they emerged in a shaded turn-of-the-century bower.

From the opposite end of the enclosed little paradise, Doug waved to them, setting bags of food down on the table. He paused long enough to throw Delaney a quick salute, then said, "Good, you're here. I've got to run. There's a gaggle of cheerleaders on some school tour who want pictures with the Barbarian Bunch." He winked at Jake. "I'll tell them you were detained."

"Thanks," Jake offered with feeling, snagging a wooden high chair from a stack positioned by the back stone wall. He set it at the foot of one of the tables and helped Caleb inside, securely fastening the belt provided.

"They have seat belts for high chairs?" Delaney asked, amazed.

Jake's glance was quick and intent. "Of course. You know how kids start climbing the minute your back is turned."

Delaney offered him a weak smile that she hoped appeared entirely knowledgeable.

Caleb began to pound on the table and squeal, holding his hands out toward the sacks and wiggling his fingers as if he could will them closer. She *had* starved him. The poor little boy was probably miserable from hunger.

"Hey, settle down."

That was all it took. One cautionary phrase from Jake, and Caleb grew quiet, folding his arms.

"That's better."

Reaching into the sacks, Jake withdrew three thick sandwiches made with hearth-baked bread, two salads and three containers of lemonade. He pushed one set toward Delaney. "Eat up."

She couldn't. Not with Caleb looking at her like that, his eyes wide and accusatory.

"Here you go, my man." Jake handed him a little container of cut vegetables, along with some sort of dip in a small plastic container. Then he proceeded to demolish another half of a sandwich, cutting it into tiny bite-size pieces and arranging them on the paper wrapping in front of the toddler. "Do you want a drink first?"

Caleb nodded, still eyeing Delaney askance.

Jake tucked his fingers into the low belt of his costume, causing Delaney's eyes to widen. But he merely withdrew a tiny Swiss army knife, which he used to cut Caleb's straw so that it was little more than an inch taller than the cup. He gave it to the toddler to drink, but kept hold of the bottom, even though it was obvious that Caleb wanted to grasp it himself.

"He can drink from a straw?" Delaney whispered, almost afraid her question might break the boy's concentration. If the idea weren't preposterous, she would have thought Caleb understood her, because he continued to glare at her with great indignation.

"Sure. It's not so different from a bottle, and sometimes it's a whole lot safer than letting him drink from a glass."

"I see." Delaney felt as if she'd said that same phrase far too often that day, but she didn't know how else to respond.

"Eat up."

He gestured toward her food, and Delaney wondered how she was going to get it past the knot that had formed in her throat.

Jake rested his forearms on the table, leaning close. "Do you want me to cut it into little pieces?"

"No!" But the protest was a bare whisper of sound. He was too close. Much too close.

"What's the matter, McBride?"

"Why do you call me that?" she demanded, side-stepping his question.

"Because you don't look like a Delaney."

"What does a 'Delaney' look like?"

"Soft and feminine."

A gasped "Oh!" escaped from her lips before she could stop it.

"There's no need to be insulted."

"And why not?" she demanded.

"I didn't say that you didn't have what it takes to become that way. It's just that every time I've seen you, you've been so... businesslike."

She cleared her throat, knowing that this was the opening she'd been waiting for all evening, and if she ignored it now, she might never divert the current direction of this conversation.

"Speaking of which, I've spoken to the agency, and to my lawyers."

"Oh?" He took a bite of his sandwich, appearing less than concerned. But he hadn't budged so much as an inch, so he was still too close to her for comfort. Much too close.

"Yes. They tell me that the contract is valid. That you are obligated to serve as Caleb's nanny for at least the next six weeks. Three, if you tender your notice."

Again, he seemed unperturbed. "So what are you going to do if I refuse?"

"Refuse? But you can't—"

"Are you going to sue me?"

"I—"

"Call the police?"

"Well—"

"Chain me up and drag me to your house?"

At that question, Delaney couldn't have forced a sound from her throat if her life depended on it. She could only blink, wondering if she'd heard him properly, as an image flashed through her head of a hot, sultry night. And this man in chains.

He set his sandwich down, inching closer and closer, much closer than she would ever have thought possible with the table between them.

"Tell me, McBride. What would you do?"

But she couldn't think. She could barely manage to breathe.

Closing her eyes, she took a deep, calming breath. "You're simply trying to rattle me."

"Is it working?"

She refused to answer. On the grounds that it would definitely incriminate her.

Opening her lashes again, she tilted her head to a proud angle. Steeling every muscle of her body, she asked frostily, "Won't you reconsider and remain as Caleb's nanny?"

"Is it only for Caleb's sake that you keep asking me?"

"What other reason could I possibly have?"

His eyes became intense, dark, nearly black. "Could you also be asking because it's something that would benefit you?"

"Of course it would. I've no idea how to properly care for a child!"

He sighed, tossing the remains of his sandwich down. "Don't you think this inexperienced-mother routine is getting a little old?"

Delaney stiffened. "I beg your pardon?"

"Look, I've seen it all. The women who cling, or cry, or just act dumb, in order to work their way up the lists at the agencies, so they don't have to care for their own kids. It's an act to get me into their house so they can—"

Delaney didn't wait to hear another word. Jumping to her feet, she reached for Caleb. "Come on, Caleb. It's time to go."

Caleb began to howl.

"Hey!"

When Jake grasped her arm, forcing her to turn and confront him, she damned the all-too-telling moisture that gathered in her eyes.

"For your information, Mr. Turk," she rasped from a tight throat, "my behavior is not an *act*. I have never had children, I have never been around children older than zygotes, and I was raised as an only child." Her voice began to rise as the frustration of the past few days broke free. "I've never even owned a *pet!* The fact that I am a woman does not endow me with innate abilities to discern what a child needs, but you, having decided you would dislike me long before you ever even met me, seem to frown upon my efforts to obtain the information I need! Well, rest assured, we won't trouble you again!''

By this time, Caleb, who had been frightened by her outburst, was crying in earnest. Delaney struggled with the safety belt around his waist, only to fumble, causing it to become hopelessly twisted.

A hand touched her shoulder, pulling her away. Then Caleb was given a drink, and his sobs, mercifully, began to die.

Sighing in defeat, Delaney leaned her hands against the polished wood of the table, closed her eyes and wished she were somewhere, anywhere, else. Why couldn't her life return to the way it had been only days before? Ordered. Busy.

Sterile.

She thrust that thought away as quickly as it came, but it could not be completely banished. Vaguely she heard Jake murmuring to Caleb, the clatter of ice as he poured half his drink into a flower bed and gave the much lighter cup back to the boy to hold himself. Then Jake's strong hands returned to clasp her arms, turn her and fold her against his chest.

"I'm sorry," she whispered, the words bursting free of their own accord. She didn't dare lift her hands to wipe at the tears that trembled on her lashes. She didn't want him to see them. She didn't want him to know she was so weak. Delaney had never been a woman who cried easily, and to do so now was galling. "I've just had a very bad day. A very bad *few* days."

"I'm sorry, too," he said, stroking her hair. "I had no idea." After a minute he continued, "An only child, hmm?"

She nodded against his chest.

"No baby-sitting experience, I take it?"

She fought the urge to laugh. By the age of nine, she'd already been enrolled in college. "No."

"Not even a hamster?"

She shook her head.

"Then I guess I owe you an apology. I suppose I pushed you a little too far with my questions. I just assumed you were—"

"Acting this stupid in order to manipulate you." She cleared her throat. "I assure you, there was no acting—and no manipulation—involved."

He drew back then, looking at her, staring deep into her eyes so that she felt as if he could see her very soul. Then he took a deep breath.

"Well, then. I guess you've pushed me into a bit of a corner, haven't you?"

Her brow furrowed. "Corner?"

"I guess you'll be getting yourself a nanny."

She didn't even dare breathe. "Really?"

"But before you agree, I want it known—for the record—that this was your idea."

"Yes, of course. Yes!"

"So we may as well spell out the rest of the details as well. I'm live-in help, McBride. If I'm going to teach you how to take care of Caleb, those arrangements will be even more necessary."

She nodded, unable to speak when she realized that if he accepted the position, there would be no escaping this man. He would help her feed, bathe and care for Caleb. All while sleeping under the same roof as her at night.

"I have every other Thursday off, as well as evenings after six—that's when I work here—but I'm back by ten."

"Of course."

"Marlene arranged for her housekeeper to care for Caleb during that time, but occasionally I brought him here. I'd like your permission to continue that practice."

"Fine."

"Unless you hire someone, you'll have to take care of him on my days off. I can't take him at all on those days, since I have other business responsibilities."

"No problem."

His hands remained on her back, large and firm and imposing. They stayed there long after the need for comfort had passed.

"Then we have ourselves a deal." He held out a hand.

Delaney hesitated only a second before allowing her own to be swallowed whole. "Yes. We have a deal.'' A jolt of sensation shot from the spot where their hands joined, making her feel oddly breathless.

Finally, just when she feared she would not be able to breathe, he backed away, returning to the picnic table.

"Forget about the crib and stuff for tonight," he said. "I'll get someone to come help you load his playpen and some of the toys into your car. Tomorrow I'll come by first thing and bring the van myself. Deal?"

"Deal."

She returned to her seat, uncomfortable at having broken down, at his having seen her like this, but Jake caught her chin, forcing her to look at him.

"But it's a temporary arrangement. Six weeks. That's all I can give you."

Six weeks.

So short a time for Caleb's needs.

But oh, so long for Delaney to deny her own.

"After that, you'll have to prove to yourself and everybody else that you can handle him on your own."

"Yes."

"Fifteen minutes, Jake!" a voice yelled from the sidewalk.

"Your next show?" she asked in a near-whisper.

"Yeah."

She gestured toward Caleb, who was happily eating his dinner, snitching cheese from Jake's sandwich and sipping lemonade in between bites.

"You'd better be going, then." She reached for her own drink so that she would have something to do with her hands. "We'll find our own way out once Caleb has finished."

As if he knew Jake was about to leave, the boy looked up, peered warily their way, and started to whimper, holding out his hands. "Ake! Ake!"

Jake touched his nose. "I'll see you tomorrow, my man."

Caleb must have understood the promise, because he smiled and returned to his food.

"You'll be okay here?" Jake asked of her.

"Yes. We'll be fine."

"What's your address, so I can bring those things? I'll drop by about eleven."

She hesitated before giving him directions. In truth, she dreaded having him see her huge mausoleum of a house in Beverly Hills. He would no doubt disapprove of it, thinking it wasn't a proper place to raise a child.

"Call me for the directions," she finally said. "I'll take the day off and meet you. That way you'll have someone to help unpack things from the truck."

His lips twitched in a quick smile. Somehow she sensed his other employers had never bothered to offer their help.

"Fine. I'll bring lunch."

He was about to leave when Delaney asked, "Do you mind if I ask you a personal question?"

His eyes—which had momentarily sparkled with amusement—became serious again. "Why did I become a nanny?" he said, before she could voice her thoughts.

"Yes."

"I like kids."

"So why not become a counselor or a teacher?"

He laughed. "Because I've never done anything that predictable."

"What do you mean?"

"I don't want to be like my father. When I was fifteen, I woke up one morning and discovered that my old man had gone for a pack of cigarettes the night before. He didn't come back."

"Your mother must have been frantic."

"I didn't have a mother. She'd died the year before. Brain tumor." It was a statement of fact, made without bitterness.

"I'm sorry."

He only shrugged. "My father couldn't handle it—or the three kids left behind. He quit his job, drank himself into a stupor—the whole situation sounds really clichéd, doesn't it? But my father was like that. He lived in a rut all his life. Never had an original idea. Even his death was clichéd. They found him two weeks later in a bus-station rest room. He'd shoved a .45 into his mouth and pulled the trigger."

Delaney stared at Jake in horror. A boy who'd been forced to become a man much too soon.

Just as she had been pushed into adulthood far too soon.

As soon as the thought raced into her head, she shoved it aside, but the empathy it brought with it could not be so easily abandoned.

"The social workers came to put us all in some sort of foster care, but I didn't want to go."

"What did you do?"

Again, the quick bark of laughter. "Everything. I rode with a biker gang, joined a band, hitchhiked cross-country—even did a stint with the merchant marine. But eventually I came back here where it all started. I took a job at a homeless shelter and studied for the GED. Pretty soon I developed a reputation for helping adolescents in trouble. I began to work one-on-one with the kids, a sort of paid companion, as I put myself through college. Soon, the kids got younger, the employers more exclusive." He glanced at Caleb. "Until this little tyke. He was the first baby I was ever hired to care for—and I liked the job. Liked it a lot."

"Then why have you been so resistant to working for me?"

"Because I knew from the very beginning that it wouldn't be right. It wouldn't be fair."

"Fair?"

"You've got two months to prove you can be his mother." He took a step closer. "If you don't, Caleb will be given to me."

The statement was so sudden, so unexpected, she felt her whole body become chill. "You're the alternate foster care?"

He nodded.

"Oh." She understood his reluctance now, his anger. But even though she understood the motivation for his emotions, she felt no better. She'd invited him into her home, would pay for his help, and he was the one person who would benefit most from her failure.

Her gaze skipped to the boy. Caleb was supposed to belong to Jake, not to her. Their relationship was already proved.

But even as she realized she'd been given a logical way out of her commitment to Marlie, she knew that she couldn't surrender. Not now. Not yet. Not when Marlie had put so much trust in her. So much faith. She'd wanted Delaney to be the mother of her child, and as much as Delaney might doubt the wisdom of such an action, she felt honor-bound to uphold it.

"There was another reason for my hesitation, McBride," Jake said.

"Oh?"

"I also knew we could never keep things strictly professional between us."

The words shuddered in the air around them, stark and heavy.

"Do you still want me to live with you, McBride? Do you still want me sleeping in your house, spending most of my time with you, knowing that I've never been one to avoid temptation too much, should it strike?"

She had to clear her throat to speak. "What about the professional ethics you recited yesterday?"

His smile was slow, heated, causing gooseflesh to rise on her arms. "I'm beginning to believe that in this case, I may have to make an exception."

How in the world could she possibly respond to that?

Finally, she croaked, "So those are the only reasons you hesitated in helping me?"

"No." His eyes became dark, grave. "There were other factors involved. Those are much more serious. I didn't want to like you, McBride. I didn't want to accept the fact Marlene had wanted you to be Caleb's guardian instead of someone like me, who's known him all his life." His eyes grew dark and serious. "I guess it's just as well that you knew that from the beginning, isn't it, Delaney?"

Her name. He'd used her first name.

But as he stood and walked away, Delaney couldn't avoid the fact that it was not the comforting detail it should have been. Instead, it caused a cool shiver of warning to trace down her spine.

Chapter Six

"Mom?"

Delaney poked her head around the doorjamb of her mother's house in Bel Air. She'd learned long ago that one did not march into her parents' abode without announcing oneself first. The chances of stumbling into some committee meeting or some outlandish kiddie-show routine were far too great.

"Mom?"

"In here, dear."

Easing inside, she tightly held Caleb's hand, leading him into the hallway and down to the library door.

"Are you busy?"

"Not at all."

But when Delaney saw what her mother was doing, she knew she should have known better than to assume that Dodie was unengaged.

Her mother stood on a carpeted dais at the far end of the room, a pair of floodlights illuminating her petite silhouette. She was swathed in a silk toga, her hair teased at least six inches from the top of her head, a mean-eyed Persian cat held in her grasp. Around her stood at least a half dozen workmen, a photographer, a woman with an enormous powder puff dangling from a string hung around her neck, and a meek, mousy woman who clutched a can of hair spray to her chest like a life preserver.

"Darling!" Dodie exclaimed. "They want to photograph me for a credit card advertisement! Isn't that the wildest thing you've ever heard?"

Any other daughter would have been surprised, Delaney supposed, but she had long since accepted the fact that her parents were eccentric. Her father—the host of a daily kiddie show that combined Howdy-Doody-type puppets with Ninja Turtlelike plots and hours and hours of cartoons—was invariably experimenting with some new costume or some new comic routine. In the meantime, Dodie flitted from one social conquest to another, scattering her charity work like diamonds in between engagements. Through it all, they'd managed to raise a child genius, their only daughter. And even with the boarding schools and prep schools and colleges that had sometimes kept them apart, they'd made Delaney feel loved.

"What do you think of the outfit, dear?"

"It's a bit...extreme."

"Isn't it *just!* I believe I'll ask if I can keep it afterward. It would be great for the benefit, don't you think?"

The benefit? The *Lexington* benefit?

"Well, Mom..." she began, feeling Caleb inch closer to her, his arms winding around her leg, as if he feared she would leave him here. It was the first time he'd turned to *her* for comfort, and it caused her heart to melt into a warm little puddle.

Smiling down at him, she ruffled the bright fluff of blond hair that tumbled over his brow. He blinked at her, his eyes as brilliantly blue as those of her mother's cat.

"I won't wear my hair like this, of course," Dodie was saying. "In my opinion, it's a little big for my face, but...what the hell. It's just an ad. Isn't it, Machiavelli?" she crooned in the cat's direction. The cat offered a low, malevolent growl that succinctly conveyed its desire to be somewhere—anywhere— else.

Caleb stared at the cat and giggled.

Judging by Machiavelli's hiss, he was not as enamored of the boy.

Delaney knelt to whisper in Caleb's ear, "What is that? A kitty? Mmm? Don't try to catch him, though. He's a mean kitty. Bad kitty."

Caleb snickered and rubbed at his nose with his hand. "Bad kitty."

"Yes, the kitty is bad."

Her mother's peal of laughter caused Delaney to look up.

"Oh, how I wish your father were here with the video camera, sweetheart."

Delaney flushed in embarrassment. She was thirty years old, but her parents still followed her with a video camera as if she were six and about to do something witty and charming.

"How absolutely *maternal* you look, dear."

"Mother—"

"You positively *glow.*"

"Isn't that sentiment reserved for pregnant women?"

Dodie wrinkled her nose becomingly. "I don't see why. I've seen that look on my own face often enough in your father's home movies. You were such an adorable creature when you were that age."

Seeking to sway her mother's attention, Delaney said, "Mother, this is Caleb."

Her mother brightened, her face scrunching up into that comical expression worn by grandmothers and people who peered into prams. "Of course it is. This is the itty-bitty Caleb I've heard so much about. Why, you're almost a man!" she said in a singsong voice. "What a delightful little baby boy you are!"

"Mother," Delaney murmured in protest, feeling the eyes of the entire production crew swinging her way.

"Now, don't you worry about them, dear. I'm sure they think he's enchanting, too. Don't you, Madge?"

The woman with the powder puff croaked, "Sure," as she took a thin cigar and a box of matches from her breast pocket. Her voice resonated with a combination of the rasp of a seasoned chain-smoker and the nasal quality of a New York cabbie. "Enchanting."

Delaney was far from relieved. She hated being the center of attention—especially in the midst of a crowd such as this.

"Mom, can I borrow the honeymoon house?"

"The honeymoon house," Dodie echoed, glancing at each of the production personnel, as if they would volunteer some sort of explanation. "What's wrong with your place, dear?"

"Nothing! Nothing." She had to be careful with what she said, otherwise her mother would take it into her head to redecorate the place or something, thinking Delaney found it uncomfortable.

Delaney's gaze bounced from the irritated photographer to Madge. "I just decided to take a little time off, and I thought I'd go somewhere with..."

"Furniture?" her mother asked wryly. "You know, that house we bought you in Beverly Hills would look much better if a person had someplace to sit. I don't care if it *was* owned by some silent-film star. I'd be more than happy to go with you. We

could take Caleb, stop and get some lunch at the Tea
Room, take in a movie."

"Yes, well, in getting back to the honeymoon
house. I thought a...smaller place might be better
for little Caleb. Until we get acquainted."

Dodie waved the explanations away. "Of course,
of course. The keys are in the cookie jar in the
kitchen. I'm delighted you'll be using the cottage.
Why, just yesterday, I was saying to your father, I
said, 'Marshall—'"

"Mrs. McBride, we really should begin filming
again," the director said, interrupting her.

Delaney took that as her cue. "I won't interrupt
you any longer, Mom. I'll call you tonight—your
idea of shopping and lunch sounds grand. Maybe
sometime next week."

"Of course, dear. Of course. Once you're settled—and don't forget I've promised your father that
I would ask you about taking little Caleb to your
father's studio and then to the canteen some afternoon. Marshall can't seem to understand that you
need some time to *bond*."

There was that word again.

"I told him there would be plenty of time—plenty
of other grandchildren to spoil—but he seems to
think that if he doesn't take the opportunity now,
this instant, it will disappear. He's waited so long,
you know," her mother added chidingly.

Delaney fought the urge to roll her eyes, knowing
that while her father might like a toddler such as

Caleb to bounce on his knee, it was Dodie who felt starved for grandchildren.

"Yes, well . . . I'll be in touch. Thanks, Mom."

Scooping Caleb into her arms, she nearly ran from the room. Hurrying to the kitchen, she sidestepped Liato, who was whacking at a chicken breast with a cleaver. Since the woman's back was to her—and Delaney knew how she hated to be disturbed in the midst of her cooking—she snagged the keys from a cookie jar filled with old buttons, then hurried outside to the Jaguar.

"You don't know how lucky we are that Mom was busy," she murmured as she secured Caleb in his car seat. Caleb just stared at her, looking quite stunned by all he'd just seen.

Delaney laughed and tickled his chin. "They're quite a bunch, aren't they?"

Was it possible for a toddler to look shell-shocked?

She chuckled again, smoothing his hair back from his face. "You'll learn to love them, Caleb," she said, then grew quite still as the meaning behind the words sank into her brain.

Was she actually considering keeping the boy? As her own child? Forever?

The questions and worries such a thought brought were overwhelming—downright terrifying.

And, looking at him now, seeing his dimpled cheeks and chubby chin, she wondered how such an awesome decision could have been foisted on her by a woman who was little more than a stranger.

Sighing, Delaney closed the door and rounded the car to her own side. She tried not to analyze why she felt so uncertain about the decisions she must shortly make—and why she found it necessary to borrow the family honeymoon house. Her own home was closer and more accessible to just about everything, but there was something about the smaller house, with its cozy furniture and well-stocked larder, that had her thinking it would be a lot easier to explain than the marble mansion she'd called home for six years.

"It will work out just fine," she said to Caleb, revving the engine.

She only wished she felt as sure as she sounded.

Because if she and Jake were to be considered candidates for parenthood, she already knew who was miles ahead of her in experience.

THE HONEYMOON HOUSE was actually the first home that her mother and father had ever owned. Although Delaney had never lived there herself, she still felt a special affection for the place. The simple four-bedroom cottage had originally been located in the heart of Los Angeles. After her father made his first million, the McBrides had bought a small parcel of land in what was then the suburbs, surrounded it with trees and a privacy fence, moved the house onto the property and allowed the city to grow around them. But even with the encroachment of society, it was incredibly private, quaint, and distinctly homey.

Driving into the small detached garage, Delaney lifted Caleb from his seat and shut the overhead door. She was just entering the cottage when the phone in her purse rang. Setting Caleb down with a murmured "Hurry inside" she quickly answered.

"Hello?"

"McBride?"

Her heart gave a little flutter when she recognized Jake's voice. "Yes."

"Are you ready to relay your directions?"

"Of course." She quickly gave him the instructions he needed.

When she'd finished, he asked, "How's Caleb this morning?"

She glanced down at the toddler, who had crawled under a glass coffee table and was staring up at a clear bowl of apples that appeared to hover in the air over his head. He'd still glared at her for most of the morning—and had a tantrum when she dressed him in jeans and a striped T-shirt—but he'd suspended his crying for an hour or two.

"Fine, I guess. I'm sure he'll feel better once you've moved in." As would she. Then she wouldn't fear she was about to warp Caleb for life with her inexpert care.

"Be there in about twenty minutes."

HE WAS THERE IN FIFTEEN.

Jake wasn't sure exactly what he'd expected of

Delaney's home, but the minute he pulled into the driveway, he knew *this* wasn't it.

The house was like something out of a fifties movie. Small, quaint, cottagelike, set back in a patch of trees amid beds of petunias and marigolds.

As he killed the engine and stepped onto the sidewalk, Delaney emerged from the front door, holding Caleb by the hand and pointing Jake's way. Jake couldn't help thinking that if she was wearing an apron and a string of pearls, she might pass for June Cleaver. Except, perhaps, for her expression. It was clear that she was nervous about the ensuing arrangements. Nervous and yet relieved. An odd combination.

Caleb squealed when he saw him and bolted forward. Swinging the boy into his arms, Jake offered him a tickle on his stomach in way of greeting, but he couldn't seem to pull his eyes away from Delaney. She'd said she'd taken the day off, but she was still dressed in a slim skirt, a silk blouse and moderate heels.

"I thought you were going to help me move."

"I am."

"Then don't you think you should put on a pair of jeans?"

She glanced down at herself, obviously nonplussed. "I, uh, don't have a clean pair," she said.

Making him wonder if she had a pair at all.

"In that case, I'll put you in charge of the boxes and toys."

"Fine."

It took little more than an hour to get everything off the truck and into the bedroom she'd set aside for Caleb. When they'd finished, Jake had to give Delaney credit. Even in her heels and skirt, she was a hard worker, refusing to balk at a job simply because a box was heavy or a piece of furniture awkward.

Padding down the quiet hallway, he paused when he heard Delaney speaking in a hushed voice.

"This is your window. See how it looks over the backyard?"

"Kitty."

"No, we don't have a kitty."

"Kitty!"

"Maybe we could borrow Machiavelli sometime, hmm?"

Jake wondered just who Machiavelli was.

"Bad kitty."

Delaney laughed. "You remember! Machiavelli is my mother's bad kitty."

Well, at least that mystery had been explained.

"Look at this, Caleb. This trunk is where we'll put your toys."

"*Oys!*" The shout was augmented by a clatter of plastic, and Jake decided it was time to make his presence known.

"I put the Harley in the garage," he said, hooking his fingers around the top of the doorjamb and leaning into the nursery.

Delaney looked up from an intense scrutiny of a toy tractor. Her hair was decidedly mussed, a lock draped over her forehead and in her eyes. That, combined with the smudge of dirt on her cheek, made her quite inviting.

"That's fine," she muttered absently. "Have you seen this thing? It makes noises. Just like a real tractor. You push this little button here and—" She broke off, clearly embarrassed. "Of course, I'm sure you already know that."

"My brother Nick gave it to him for his birthday."

She rose to her feet, brushing her hands on her skirt. "What now?" she asked. After a glance at the baby, who was playing with a set of oversize cars, she gave her attention to Jake.

"I need to return the truck. Why don't you and Caleb follow in your car? We'll grab something to eat, then you can drop me off at my Jeep. I've already got my things loaded inside it. That way, I'll be completely moved."

She nodded, a tight little smile pursing her lips. When she would have brushed past him, he stopped her, crowding her against the wall. He'd give her one more chance to back out of the agreement, test her to the limit.

"You haven't changed your mind, have you?"

"About what?" The question was breathy. Unconsciously erotic.

"My coming to work here." He prayed that she would say she had, that she would send him packing.

Then, inexplicably, he prayed she would let him stay. It didn't matter that they shouldn't be together while vying for Caleb's custody. He wanted to be here. With her. With Caleb. With them both.

"No." Again, so breathy. So delightful. She was such a curious mixture of innocence and tempered steel.

"You're sure? You seem a little uncomfortable." And he didn't mind pointing out the fact, because it obviously made her even more uncomfortable.

She cleared her throat, tucking a silky lock of hair behind her ear. "Caleb is already much more relaxed, having you near."

"I wasn't talking about Caleb." With his thumb, he brushed at the smudge of dirt on her cheek, and she jumped as if he'd touched her with a hot brand.

"Do *you* still want me to stay?"

Her lips trembled in a way that was unconsciously inviting. Seductive.

"Yes, of course."

"Good."

Jake knew he should back away. He knew he should keep his distance, especially now, on the first day in her employ. But he couldn't resist. He had to see if she still tasted as good as he remembered.

The moment his lips closed over her own, he knew that he hadn't been mistaken. She was still so sweet, so hesitant, so tempting. The mere scent of her—with its hint of soap and some expensive perfume—went straight to his gut. So much so that he couldn't prevent the way his arms slipped around her waist and he drew her closer, closer, until she was pressed tightly against him.

There was only a moment's hesitation on her part before she grew still, her fingers curling into his T-shirt and clutching him in a way that caused his groin to burn. Never in his life had a woman responded to him like this. With such hesitancy and simplicity.

His arms immediately tightened, the embrace growing more urgent, more demanding. He pushed her against the doorway, leaning into her, needing to feel her breasts flatten against him, the quick intake of her breath, the slender span of her waist. Then his hands were moving to her hair, dragging it from its moorings and sinking into its silky softness.

Dear heaven above, why did she keep it pinned up like some maiden aunt, when it was so rich, so vibrant, so delightful to hold?

He slanted his head and slid his tongue into her mouth, tasting her intimately. He felt her shudder against him. Felt her wrap her arms around his neck and pull him closer.

Breaking away, he touched his lips to her ear, her jaw, her neck. Then, summoning more control than he'd ever known he possessed, he forced himself to back away. When she gazed up at him with wide, dark eyes, he traced her lips with his finger.

"Too much too soon can be dangerous" was his only explanation. He knew that if he didn't draw away now, he never would. Considering the circumstances, all the obstacles that would continue to keep them apart, *not* drawing away would be the worst thing he could do.

She turned away from him, pressing her fingers to her lips. "Wouldn't it be better for both of us, all around, if we made sure that nothing of this sort happened?"

"Maybe." He grasped her shoulders. "But I've always enjoyed taking a walk on the wild side, living on the edge. I tend to do things my own way."

"And what way is this?"

"The way it has to be." His grip tightened ever so slightly, as he sensed the truth of that reply before he spoke it. That if Caleb *was* to be left in this woman's care, it would be to the person he sensed hidden away inside her. The gentle one. The passionate one.

She stood so still, so proud, so obviously confused.

He eased closer, bending to whisper in her ear. "Was it really so bad? To be kissed?"

"No."

"Then we won't worry about it." He released her to take her hand, weaving their fingers together. "Because it will happen again. On that, you can rely."

BUT IT DIDN'T. Not for some time.

Bit by bit, Jake eased into Delaney's life, much the same way Caleb was doing. To her infinite surprise, it was Jake who cooked their breakfast each morning and supplied Delaney with a lunch. She supposed it was a bit of a joke at first. He bought her a "Sesame Street" lunch box after she sat entranced over an opera segment adapted from *Aida* for the children's show. When she brought the container back empty the first few days, he continued with the practice until she began to look forward to the thick sandwiches, miniature containers of pudding, vegetable sticks and juice.

Each evening, Jake led her through what he called his "tutoring" sessions. After living with her for only a week, Jake realized she didn't know the difference between Barney and children's vitamins, so he'd taken it upon himself to educate her in everything a new mother needed to know. From child safety caps to cartoons.

Through it all, Caleb was beginning to relax around her. He no longer screamed when Jake left for work. She'd learned how to master Fisher-Price toys and the peanut butter sandwich. So much so that she was beginning to believe she might, just might, be able to cope with having a child in her life. More than that, she was beginning to think she might learn to enjoy the experience. What worried her now was the fact that once Jake left them, it might not be

Caleb who would react most strongly to his absence.

A knock on the door brought her head up from the storybook she held, and she kissed the top of Caleb's head.

"Who could that be, hmm?" Outside, the street was dark, save for the porch light and a distant street lamp.

It was late, far past Caleb's bedtime, but she'd allowed him to stay up with her, to coax her into reading another story, because for the first time he seemed content with her company. Hers and hers alone.

Since it was Thursday, Jake had disappeared for an evening out and she'd been left to care for the toddler on her own. Delaney had regarded the evening as a test of sorts, to see if she was getting the hang of motherhood. She'd been surprised at how pleasant it could be to spend the day with him. The familiar rituals of bathtime and naptime and dinnertime had taken on even more significance because she'd accomplished them on her own.

"Do'," Caleb whispered, pointing to the front door.

"Yes. Someone has come to see us."

She set Caleb on the floor, and he immediately ran to the window, standing on tiptoe in his footed pajamas to peek outside.

Delaney was equally careful, peering through the peephole, then grinning in delight.

"It's your grandpa!"

The moment the words came from her mouth, she wished she could bring them back. By speaking them aloud, she was revealing far too much to herself. The way she was "bonding" with the boy, just as her mother had claimed she would. Bonding, hell. She was beginning to adore him, and such emotions were dangerous at best.

Yanking open the door, she sought to bury her misgivings in action.

"Dad!" she cried, and, seeing the smaller woman with him, carrying a casserole dish, she offered more uncertainly, "Mom?"

"Hello, dear," Dodie said, breezing inside and bringing with her the exotic scent of her own secret lasagna recipe. "We won't stay, but Marshall insisted on meeting Caleb. Absolutely *insisted.*"

Judging by the twinkle in Marshall's eye, the statement was utter balderdash, but he didn't correct his wife.

"We knew you'd be hungry," Dodie continued without stopping, making her way to the kitchen, her voice wafting behind her, "so I brought a little something."

"Mom, it's eight o'clock."

"That doesn't mean you should avoid the urge to eat when you're hungry," her mother said, reappearing. "You're too thin, you know. I doubt you've eaten a square meal in a month."

A statement that would have been true before Jake moved in and took over the cooking.

Dodie paused in the doorway and clapped her hands, bending low and opening her arms. "There's our little man! Come give Nana Dodie a big hug!"

Nana Dodie. It was a bit too close to another word for *Grandma* for Delaney's comfort, but after glancing her way, Caleb surprised them all by toddling toward Dodie and allowing himself to be scooped into her embrace.

"Kitty!"

Dodie laughed. "He remembers me. How charming." Rocking him close, she said to her husband, "We must see about finding our little man a kitten, Marshall."

"Yes, dear." Marshall reached out to squeeze Delaney's shoulder. "And how's our 'little' girl?"

She wrapped her own arm around his waist. "Great, Daddy. Just great."

"You're sure."

"Yes."

"So the little tyke hasn't worn you out yet?"

"No."

"She has help, Marshall. I told you that," Dodie said, bouncing a giggling Caleb and making clopping sounds as she approached. "It's ... *clippety-clop* ... a *man* ... *clippity-clop* ... "

"I know that, Dodie. You've told me that often enough." He patted Delaney's arm. "I just wanted to make sure that the arrangement was working for you.''

How sweet. Her father had always been her champion, but it touched her to see that even after all these years, he was concerned about her safety and welfare.

''Yes, Dad. He's wonderful with Caleb—and he's already taught me so much.''

''That I can see.''

As her father perused the room, Delaney saw it fresh, through his eyes—the clutter of children's toys, the television still turned to a Muppet video, a blanket tossed over the arm of a couch.

''I like what you've done with the place, Delaney.''

Dodie laughed, causing Caleb to stare at her in wonder, then chuckle himself. Then she sighed. ''I wish we could stay.''

''We're on our way to a preview of the rough cut of her commercial.''

Dodie handed Caleb to Delaney. ''They wouldn't have allowed such a thing, of course, except that your father and I are filthy rich and they're hoping for a donation during their Christmas charity drive.''

''Mother!''

''Well, it's true. Why be coy?'' She leaned forward to kiss Caleb on the cheek. ''We'll see you soon, Pumpkin.''

Marshall reached out to solemnly shake the boy's hand. "I hope you'll come to visit me at the studio sometime this week?"

Caleb nodded, even though he couldn't possibly know what Marshall meant.

Marshall stroked Delaney's cheek next. "Make sure you get your rest."

"I will, Dad."

Then they were gone, Dodie rushing to the car as if it were a carriage about to transport her to a ball.

As they waved and threw kisses, Delaney felt her first real sense of something being "right" about this whole situation. Delaney might not be the most expert of mothers yet, but she had something that Jake could not offer the boy.

A pair of doting grandparents.

So why did the thought of denying Jake his own claim to Caleb make her feel so mean?

Chapter Seven

Delaney stepped into the reception room to her office and noiselessly closed the door behind her. "I don't suppose they called about what kind of trade-in they'd give me on the Jaguar, did they?"

Her expensive pumps had made no sound on the thick carpet, and Linda jumped, splaying a hand over her heart.

"Geez, I wish you wouldn't do that."

"Do what?"

"Sneak up on a person. It isn't natural, I tell you. Don't you ever make any noise?"

Delaney fought a small smile. "Never. It's not in my job description. What about the Jaguar?"

Linda lifted a note from her blotter and waggled it in front of Delaney. "According to the manager, they'd be willing to give you this much if you trade it in on another Jag."

"I don't want another one. It's murder to use with a car seat."

Linda grinned. "A car seat, hmm? Don't you think it's a little premature to change your car before you've been given full custody?"

It was. It was an incredibly risky move. But she felt compelled to do it all the same. How could she explain to her secretary that her attitude had changed so quickly? That only weeks ago she'd been interested in little more than her work, and now she wished she didn't have to come to work at all?

Perhaps the whole situation was still new. Perhaps she'd soon grow tired of it all.

But what scared her most was that she didn't think she would.

She enjoyed her time with Caleb. She loved his baby giggles and the scent of his freshly washed skin. She was entranced by his toys, the games he made up to entertain himself, the new words he learned every day.

Sighing at her own giddy thoughts, Delaney took the proffered note and moved into her personal office. Linda followed her like a loyal bloodhound. "Burt said to tell you he wouldn't be back in the office until Thursday. He's got those in-service meetings."

"Fine." Tossing the lab coat over her leather-tufted chair in an unaccustomed display of untidiness, Delaney grasped her briefcase and set it on the desk. Flicking the catch, she opened the attaché and shoved a computer printout on top of a copy of *Cat in the Hat* and a child-development text Jake had loaned her. She could read them all tonight, after Jake left for his job at Twin Towers and Caleb had taken his bath.

Slamming the lid closed and throwing the latches, she stepped into the bathroom, quickly retouching her makeup and repinning her hair in its artful sweep. Then she returned to her office.

"Where are you going tonight? Some hot date?"

Knowing Linda wouldn't give up until she had the truth, Delaney answered, "No. I'll be spending the evening with Caleb."

"How's it progressing?"

"Fine, I suppose. He doesn't scream at me anymore."

"And how's the nanny?" Linda had taken a newer and even more relentless interest in Jake Turk after learning just what he did at Twin Towers. When she discovered that he'd moved into Delaney's house, she'd been agog with curiosity.

"This is what? Your fifth night?"

"A full week tomorrow."

"Hmm..."

At Linda's murmur, Delaney looked up.

"What?"

"Nothing. Nothing."

"Linda..."

The redhead didn't bother to answer, but swept into the outer office.

"Have a good time. Oh! Those tapes you ordered arrived. I put them on the end of the counter."

"Great!" Delaney peered beneath the open flap, noting in satisfaction that the bookstore had been able to find her a selection of "Sesame Street" recordings. Jake had insisted she begin collecting audiotapes and videotapes that would aid Caleb's education. Lately, whatever Jake told her to do, she did.

Even though she couldn't bear to bring herself to think what Jake would do, how he would feel, if she was successful in her endeavors and Caleb remained with her.

Just thinking about separating the two of them gave her heart a little wrench. She'd tried to remind herself that she was his employer. Nothing more. Nothing less.

In all honesty, the inner warning was needless. In the past few days, she'd behaved as professionally as a middle-aged schoolmarm. She'd worn her severest suits, scraped her hair back into a tight, restrictive knot and spoken in a brisk and no-nonsense tone. From the moment she arrived home each night until Jacob Turk walked out the door for Twin Towers, it was obvious that she had one thing in mind.

Caleb's welfare.

But, the little voice whispered in return, that didn't seem to stop her from stealing glances at Jake when he bent over to wipe Caleb's face, or when he stretched his arms overhead and yawned. Like a man replete...

Yanking her mind away from such thoughts, Delaney threw Linda a distracted wave and strode outside, nearly gasping at the sudden heat of the afternoon after a day spent in an air-conditioned building. Slipping into the car, she automatically turned the key and glanced at her reflection in the rearview mirror.

Professional.

From the taupe pumps she wore to her matching suit and blouse, no one could have faulted her appearance. No one could have faulted her behavior, either. She was a professional first, a woman second.

Even if she didn't want to be.

The thought ricocheted through her mind with the strength of a pistol shot. Her fingers tightened around the wheel. Reaching out, she flipped on the air-conditioning, but not even the blast of air could settle the restlessness blooming within her.

She couldn't help remembering how she'd helped Jake to bathe Caleb that morning. The day had already been hot. By the time she made her excuses to leave for work, a light sheen of sweat had settled over Jake's skin—one that had nothing to do with baby oil. His hair, which had been drawn back in its customary queue, had become slightly damp near his scalp. When he stood, a rivulet of sweat had eased from his temple, moving slowly, ever so slowly, down the strong line of his jaw before finally plunging down the side of his neck. Delaney had nearly been overcome with the urge to reach out and wipe it away.

Delaney took a deep, shuddering breath, trying to push aside the faint fluttering of her stomach. She shouldn't feel this way about Jacob Turk—especially when he had the power to take Caleb away.

Such thoughts were wrong.

Natural.

Base.

Delicious.

Groaning aloud at her own inner arguments, Delaney shoved a tape into the console, hoping the soothing strains of Beethoven would drive the disturbing thoughts from her head. When the pounding elemental rhythms of an old Eurythmics tune filled the air, it was nearly her undoing. The husky words *sweet dreams are made of this* met her ears, and she quickly hit the eject button. Linda must have exchanged the cassettes as a joke.

She drove the rest of the way home in tormenting silence. The path through the twisting avenues was becoming second nature to her now, and she slipped beneath the familiar oak trees, parking by the front path. Taking a deep breath, she closed her eyes, willing a calm reserve to fill her veins and still the delicious anticipation she felt each time she met Jacob Turk.

A soft knock on her window brought her head up. Her eyes flew open, and her heart slammed against the wall of her chest. Turning, she glanced at the man who had somehow managed to fill each of her waking moments, both consciously and unconsciously, for nearly a week now.

And he had no idea.

He opened her car door and offered her his hand. Delaney hesitated, stunned that he had come in search of her here. The past few nights, she'd tried to make sure that there was no physical contact between them. None. Yet here he stood, so close that she could smell the clean scent of his soap. His hand was outstretched, broad and warm and so very inviting.

Without allowing herself to think much beyond that point, she rested her palm in his own and swung her feet to the pavement. She felt his gaze against the bare expanse of her knees just before she straightened. For a moment, their bodies brushed, hard against soft, male against female. Then Delaney stepped away, and Jake retrieved her briefcase.

Gathering what remained of her tattered self-control, Delaney walked a few feet away, to wait by the hood of the car until Jake joined her.

For a moment, neither of them moved. Instead, they watched each other with quiet eyes. The heavy summer air settled around them with a vibrant heat.

"Hi."

Jake's voice touched her skin like a tangible caress. Low, and dark, and sweet. His gaze slipped from the smooth twist of her hair to the rounded tips of her shoes in a way that was so totally male that she couldn't help feeling completely feminine.

"Hi."

"I've got the night off."

"Oh?"

"Electrical problems at the pavilion. They canceled the show."

"I see."

Watching her, Jake gave Delaney time to gather her composure. She stood so still, so wary, like a frightened doe. She'd worn a silk suit again—he'd never known one woman could own so many. Stylish, sexless, tailored garments in somber colors and rigid lines. His gaze lifted to her face. Not for the first time, he noted the stiff pride and rigid professionalism that tainted her features.

As well as the faint tinge of panic.

She knew he could take Caleb away, she knew he could purposely alienate the boy's affections from her. And yet she kept him here, so that they both walked a dangerous tightrope. One that stretched between Caleb's custody and . . .

And what? A personal relationship between them?

As much as he wanted to deny such a possibility, he couldn't. Not from the moment he'd touched her, kissed her. But even then, he'd felt such a mix of confusing feelings. As much as he loved Caleb, could he take him from this woman? Especially when he'd seen how the boy had begun to change her. Soften her . . .

Did Delaney McBride ever laugh? Jake found himself wondering. He'd seen her smile—with a shy tilting of her mouth that was gone before he was really sure he'd seen it at all.

But he'd never heard her laugh.

Caleb trundled out the open door of the house and whooped at them from the front porch. He'd brought a toy dump truck with him, and he paused to grasp a handful of dirt from one of the planters on the porch. Then he sank to his knees with this new plaything. After a quick glance to ensure the boy was fine and involved with his chore, Jake returned his attention to the woman in front of him.

"Is something wrong?" Delaney glanced down at herself, as if she had some unsightly stain that no one had bothered to point out to her.

Jake shook his head. "No. You look fine. Great, in fact."

Too much so. It was becoming increasingly difficult for Jake to remind himself that he shouldn't become involved with this woman, shouldn't allow himself to become tempted by her presence. He could never offer her anything but a transitory relationship.

But each time they met, his resolve seemed to stretch a little thinner.

"Shall we go in?" Wanting to bring his inspection to a halt, Delaney gestured toward the front door and turned toward the grass. She walked briskly, but Jake fell easily into step beside her, his free hand automatically reaching out to rest in the hollow of her back. Despite the heat of the afternoon and the sheltering layers of her clothing, Delaney felt his touch as keenly as if it were a forbidden caress.

At the front porch, she bent to pick Caleb up. After an initial bout of squirming, he allowed her to hold him and even took an interest in the button-shaped earrings she wore.

Once again, Jake paused and glanced at her, a frown creasing his brow. Each glance made her more conscious of the way the boxy jacket she wore didn't entirely disguise the curves of her breasts or the fullness of her hips.

"Is something wrong?" Her hand lifted to touch her hair in a self-conscious gesture.

"No, it's just..." He cleared his throat. "My sister Yvette sent over some supper. She and her husband just opened up a little diner in Orange County."

"Oh?"

"She was visiting earlier and brought the stuff. She says we need to keep up our strength, with a toddler in the house."

Delaney's lips tilted in a quick smile, and she tickled Caleb under the chin, making him squeal. "I am beginning to understand what she means by that."

Once again, he paused and stared at her. He opened his mouth, hesitated, then asked, "Do you mind if I ask you a personal question?"

She stiffened slightly. "No. What?"

"Do you always dress that way? Or is this for my benefit?"

Delaney's stomach fluttered. How had he guessed?

"What's wrong with the way I dress?"

"No offense, but you look like you're going to a funeral or a power lunch."

"I came straight from work."

"But you don't change into anything more comfortable when you get here."

"My wardrobe is rather limited, since I work at a research laboratory."

"Ah, that explains it. At a place like that, they must make you dress up every day."

Her lips twitched. "Loincloths would probably be frowned upon."

"Pity."

"The institute doesn't really mandate what its employees should wear."

"Then you must be bucking for a promotion, with all those suits you have."

One of her brows lifted inquiringly.

"All that dress-for-success stuff." He lifted a hand before she could speak. "Don't get me wrong, I believe firmly in the technique. It's just that I've spent most of my life working outdoors or in body shops or gyms. I tend to feel a little strangled in a tie."

Strangled. In one word, he'd managed to sum up the way she'd felt for the past year. Sweet heaven, why hadn't she seen herself what was happening to her? Why hadn't she noticed the way she'd dug herself deeper and deeper into a rut, until she'd forgotten that there were people who enjoyed life, who wore jeans and danced?

People like Jake Turk.

He glanced at her again, then suddenly reached out to take her hand. "Come on."

Chapter Eight

"Where are we going?" Delaney asked breathlessly when he led her directly toward his bedroom.

"You need to change."

"Why?"

"Because Yvette sent marinated chicken, baked beans and potato salad, and you'll get that outfit all dirty. Besides, you give me the willies dressed like that. You look like Mrs. Beatlemeyer, my ninth-grade science teacher. She could fix the evil eye on a person from a hundred yards, and I got more than my share of the eye."

Delaney glanced regretfully at the suit she wore. For the first time in years, she found herself longing to wear something comfortable, casual, well-worn and sloppy. Sighing inwardly, she realized she didn't have anything that fit such a description.

"I'll loan you something of mine. That way, you can change into something slouchy," he offered again.

"No. This is fine." It wasn't. Even as she demurred, she felt trapped. Stifled.

"I won't take no for an answer."

She knew the truth of that statement as soon as he made it. Sighing in surrender, she threw her hands into the air. "Fine! Whatever you say!"

He steered her toward his closet. In an instant, Delaney realized she was in trouble. He laid his hands on her shoulders, pulling her tightly against him. "Let's see... Jeans? A T-shirt?"

"Your own special uniform?"

"Don't knock it until you've tried it."

"I don't think I should—"

He stopped her by turning her in his arms and taking her hands, pressing them against his chest.

Caleb had followed them into the room and now gazed at them both with wide, startled eyes. The dump truck he'd been playing with was clutched to his chest and dirt dribbled down his front and onto the floor, but at that instant, Delaney didn't care.

Jake's gaze suddenly became curious and gentle. "I want you to relax. I get the feeling you don't relax much. You seem a little uptight when we're together."

Uptight? He didn't know the half of it.

"Maybe if you change out of that suit, you'll feel more comfortable around me."

More comfortable, perhaps. More comfortable around him? She doubted it.

She saw the way Jake seemed to hesitate, his eyes growing even darker as he glanced at her hair, her face. Her lips.

Her breathing grew slightly erratic. How could a man excite her with a glance alone?

But then, he had a way of studying her that was almost tangible. A tacit, if invisible, caress.

"You look like you think I'm going to hit you," he murmured, his mouth twitching in the beginnings of a smile.

She shook her head. "No."

"Yes." He reached out to stop the side-to-side motion of her head, and his finger lingered there. "You do."

Strong and faintly calloused. Even the brief touch told her so much about him. He evidently worked hard—had two or even three jobs, from what she surmised. Yet he still had the power to be gentle. Or playful.

He sighed. "Do you know that I've spent the last few days telling myself I shouldn't do this?"

"Ethics?"

"Ethics be damned. I didn't think it would be fair to you. I'm not the kind of man you should get involved with. I'm the sort who likes a fast motorcycle, warm leather, and pushing things to the limit. You like lists and schedules and opera." He sighed, leaning forward so that his breath caressed her cheek. "But I don't want to be good anymore. I don't want to think about the future. I don't want to think about custody hearings or deal in 'what-ifs.' I want to see what Delaney McBride is like under all those layers of respectability."

The finger on her chin slipped to a point below her jawline, causing a shiver of delicious friction. Before she really comprehended his intent, he applied a gentle pressure that brought her face toward his own.

He didn't kiss her. Instead, he brushed her cheek with his mouth as he bent to whisper in her ear, "You know...*fun* is not a four letter word—and contrary to popular belief, spending time with a man can be fun." When she didn't respond, he inquired, "Delaney, can you come out and play?"

Delaney gazed at him in confusion.

His own expression grew thoughtful, his eyes dark. "You don't even know what I'm talking about, do you?"

She shook her head.

Jake took a deep breath, studying her intently. Once again, he was struck by the almost tangible wall of seriousness that surrounded Delaney McBride. Life seemed to be a business to her in many ways. Moving from point A to point B with as few obstacles as possible.

But Jake had encountered more than his share of obstacles in life. Through it all, he'd discovered that sometimes a bump or two in the road made all the effort worthwhile.

"Ake. Ake!"

They were both drawn back to reality when a little body squirmed between them and Caleb pummeled Jake's thighs with his fists, thinking he'd been left out of some new game.

As Jake drew back, he allowed his finger one last stolen caress of the velvety texture of her skin. Delaney McBride was too beautiful to be so serious.

Taking a pair of jeans and a cotton shirt from his closet, he stuffed them in her arms, then added a leather belt. "There. Go get changed." Then he lifted Caleb into his arms so that she couldn't shove the clothes back at him.

But she didn't refuse. She turned to make her way to her own bedroom. And as he watched her go, Jake wondered if their arrangement might prove an asset for the both of them.

Regardless of how this whole custody mess turned out, she could give him a few more weeks with Caleb.

And he could teach her how to laugh.

THERE WAS SOMETHING completely unnerving about wearing another person's clothes, Delaney thought as she slid into Jake's jeans. She tried not to think that he had worn these pants sometime in the none-too-distant past, that his body had warmed them, stretched the fabric taut.

Stop it!

She had to admit that the outfit *was* more comfortable than her suit. The shirt was sizes too big, the pants were loose and baggy on her slender frame. But there was something freeing about the ensemble. As if she had shed far more than her work clothes.

As she moved out of the bathroom, Delaney allowed herself one quick glance in the mirror. That glance was far from reassuring. In her opinion, she still looked staid. Staid and only slightly less uncomfortable.

Frowning, she tightened the belt one more notch and stepped into the living room. Jake was waiting for her, leaning against the rear portion of the couch, his arms crossed over his chest. Caleb stood on the cushions behind him, bracing his elbows on the back, his own features creased in an all-too-adult scowl.

"Well?" she asked, holding her arms out. "Do I pass?"

"What do you think, squirt?"

Caleb peered up at him, then at Delaney, obviously confused about the matter at hand, but wanting to participate nonetheless.

Jake eyed her critically, his chocolate-colored eyes warm and intent as they traveled from the top of her head to the tip of her toes.

"I suppose it will have to do on such short notice. Even so, I think you should..."

Before she knew what he meant to do, he'd unerringly found the pins holding her hair in place. Snatching them free, he raked his fingers through her hair, then, in a flurry of fingers, caused it to stand away from her face in a bushy mass.

"Better, much better," he murmured, taking her by the hand. Scooping Caleb up in one strong arm, he made his way outside, instructing Delaney to close the door as they passed through. To her surprise, she saw that Caleb's safety seat and a wicker basket had already been put in the Jeep. Seeing this, Caleb clapped his hands in delight and shouted, "Bye-bye! Go!"

"Where are we going?" Delaney asked.

"On a picnic."

She came to a skidding halt. "I can't go out in public dressed like this!" she exclaimed as Jake strapped Caleb into the car seat.

"Why not?" Jake demanded. Hooking the last buckle, he turned to face her, his hands on his hips. "Every woman over the age of seven is in the same kind of getup. It's the latest fad, you know."

"But I'm *not* seven. I'm thirty."

He leaned close, whispering, "So learn to adapt."

When she continued to balk, he said coaxingly, "Come on, McBride. Live a little on the wild side."

"Like you, I suppose."

"Someday I just might frighten you by showing you how much I've done just that. Now get in the Jeep."

Her chin lifted to a militant angle. "And if I don't?"

"I'll put you there myself."

It wasn't an idle threat, and she knew it.

Stiffly she climbed into her seat, automatically reaching up to tame the wild mass of her hair. When Jake shot her a stern glance, she compromised, braiding it instead.

Sighing, Jake shot Caleb a thumbs-up sign. "Let's eat!"

For the first time in as long as she could remember, Delaney chuckled softly to herself, causing Jake to smile in secret satisfaction.

It was a start. A damned good start.

"DID YOU AND CALEB have a productive morning?" Delaney asked a few minutes later as the wind whistled around them.

Jake nodded his head. "He helped me move some equipment."

"Equipment?"

He glanced at her, obviously measuring the extent of her curiosity, then said, "I've been offered a job in Washington, D.C. Some of my things are being shipped out this week."

A wave of panic gripped her heart, and her stomach felt as if she were trapped in a sinking elevator. "Oh?" she inquired, as casually as she could. "The agency said you weren't taking any new positions as a nanny."

He shrugged. "I thought a change of venue would do me good. All that atmosphere should help me with my latest project."

"What will you be doing? Working in a gym? With exercise equipment?"

He drew his eyes away from the road long enough to glance at her. For some inexplicable reason, Delaney sensed that she had disappointed him.

"No. Nothing at all like that."

"I merely thought—"

When she tried to explain her assumptions, he waved her comments aside. "It's all right. A lot of people think that my only interest is in lifting weights and building muscle."

"I didn't mean—"

"It's okay, Delaney."

After some time, he glanced at her again, his eyes near black, and a little sad. "Maybe I should show you."

He turned onto a freeway on-ramp and made his way north. Delaney didn't say anything more, afraid that she had offended him with her comments, and that if she said anything else, she would only make things worse.

In time, she began to recognize that they were on their way to Nick's house. When he pulled into the tree-shaded driveway and killed the engine, she wondered why he had brought her there.

Still, he didn't speak, didn't move. He gazed consideringly into space for a while, focusing on some distant point.

"Come on."

After unfastening Caleb, he led her toward the garage, of all places. She wondered if that was where he stored his latest "project." His body was still taut with tension, but she couldn't tell if it was because of what she'd said or because of what he was about to show her.

Slipping a key into the lock of the side entrance, he motioned for her to go inside first.

"Welcome to my workshop."

"Workshop?"

"Nick has been kind enough to rent me his garage for the last few years—for a nominal fee, of course."

"Of course."

Delaney was astonished as she stepped into the cool shadows. The interior had been transformed into a studio of sorts, with huge skylights, Formica-topped tables and shelves of equipment.

"This is what I do when I'm not Caleb's nanny or Tar the Barbarian."

Jacob touched her back, leading her toward a wall of mannequins laden with every sort of armor, uniforms, and weaponry imaginable.

"I restore these for museums all over the world. Before shipping them back to their proper homes, I make copies of the patterns necessary to recreate the basic structures of each piece. I then add a little of my own imagination, or the styles of a certain era, and build a new set that would be true to the period. A lot of my reconstructed pieces are then purchased by universities, theaters and moviemakers."

Delaney's eyes widened. "So this is how you spend your time off."

"Usually. Some of the smaller items I can carry with me. I work on them while Caleb is napping."

As if the sound of his own name had stirred him into action, Caleb wriggled and grunted until he was allowed to get down. It was obvious he'd been here before, because he made his way to a box in the corner, upending it and spilling plastic blocks onto the floor.

Since Caleb was occupied, Delaney felt free to explore.

"I've seen these before—this exact one!" she whispered reverently, reaching out to stroke one of the pieces of chain mail on a dummy that had been dressed in complete armor with a blue-and-red tabard—a poncholike garment draped over the head and belted at the waist. Delaney remembered studying such things in her history classes. "It was in that British Shakespearean movie that came out a few years ago."

He nodded. "I've always liked that piece. Luckily, the company only rented it, so I have a bit of a souvenir."

She moved on to look at a Civil War uniform— new, but carefully distressed—an obviously antique warbonnet, a quiver of brittle-looking arrows.

"You can pick it up."

"I don't dare."

"They're stronger than they look."

She fingered one, then another, feeling the scratchy turkey feathers and the wood, grown smooth from use. Next she moved on to a tray of medals and a box of coins.

"What are these?"

"Replicas of some coins I cleaned and restored for a maritime museum in New Zealand. In this box are the original coins I carved for a museum in Louisiana during their Mardi Gras exposition."

His large hands looked incongruous next to the slender pieces. Taking one, he placed it in her palm. The object was surprisingly heavy.

"You made these? How?"

"I took a lump of clay and carved away anything that didn't look right," he responded with a wry grin. "Then I cast it and made a mold. This was one of a limited edition made for collectors."

Her eyes widened. She knew she was being obvious in her surprise, but she couldn't seem to come to terms with the fact that this man, this strong, vital, vibrant man, did something so painstaking, so detailed, so...

Beautiful.

She studied the coin nestled in her hand. On its face was an intricate castle with a carved portcullis, turrets, and the details of individual stones. "There's even a dragon," she murmured, seeing the creature's head arching from one of the tower windows.

"Every castle has its dragon, don't you think? Just like every place of paradise must have its snake."

The statements struck her as being philosophical, and she looked up at him then, wondering how he had become so observant, so wise.

"Why is that, do you suppose? Why must there always be a taste of the bad?"

She was immediately reminded of the fact that Jake would leave soon. Either with Caleb or without him. Either way, the parting would be painful. For both of them. Especially after all that had occurred between them lately. The way they'd been able to interact as a . . .

Family?

That thought alone had the power to make her weak. Because it would end. It had to end. And someone would be hurt in the process.

Jake must have sensed a portion of her feelings. "Maybe the bad helps us to appreciate the good."

She couldn't hold his gaze, and was forced to focus instead on the castle. "What if there's more bad than good?"

She didn't know why she pursued the conversation, why she pushed it into areas Jake had probably never intended for it to go. But standing here, in the midst of his art, she felt . . .

Like a failure.

The thought was ludicrous. She had so much—a challenging career, a beautiful home, a nice car.

But those were just *things*. They didn't really matter as much as . . .

Children.

Relationships.

Not being alone.

Jake tipped her chin up so that he could look at her.

"Why so sad all of a sudden?"

Delaney was struck by the fact that Jacob Turk would never want a woman like her—one who felt more attuned to statistics than to emotions. He needed a woman as vibrant as he.

He raised a brow, still waiting for an answer to his question. She shook her head, refusing to respond, but he wouldn't let her get away with such cowardice.

"Are there dragons in Delaney McBride's life?"

A tightness gripped her throat. "I suppose." She tried her best to make her answer seem casual, disinterested. "As you said, we all have to take the bad, as well as the good."

She placed the coin back on the worktable, but when she would have turned away, he stopped her.

"So what do you do when they roar, Delaney?"

Her brow furrowed in confusion.

"How do you relieve the stress—shop, go to the movies, sunbathe?"

"I work."

"That's a lousy solution."

"It takes my mind off things."

"You need to lighten up, McBride."

Speechless, Delaney stared at him.

He looked at her long and hard. Before she knew what he meant to do, he retrieved the coin and handed it to her.

"This is yours."

She gasped. "I couldn't possibly—"

"It's not a gift, Delaney. It's a talisman."

He walked to the door, taking Caleb by the hand, and waited, making it quite clear that he meant for them to leave. As she stepped into the searing heat and he relocked the garage, she demanded, "What do you mean, it's a talisman?"

He looked so strong, so invincible, standing there with a child clutching his hand. A child who needed a man in his life.

Just as much as he needed a mother.

"You're to take it home, put it by your bed. Each night before you go to sleep, I want you to look at it and ask yourself, 'What did I do today that gave me pleasure?'"

Pleasure.

The word throbbed between them, heavy with unspoken intent. Then Jake swung Caleb into his arms and strode toward the car.

Leaving her to wonder how there could ever be any pleasure knowing the decision each of them must face some time soon.

"BEFORE YOU GO TO SLEEP, I want you to look at it and ask yourself, 'What did I do today that gave me pleasure?'"

The words echoed through Delaney's head much later that evening, when she and Jake returned to carry a sleeping Caleb into his room.

Jake's footsteps were noiseless as he padded up the staircase to the long hall that stretched from one end of the house to the other, French doors at either end leading out to balconies the size of postage stamps.

The excursion they'd taken had been surprisingly serene. Peaceful. She and Jake had sat at the picnic benches at Hoover Park, watching Caleb play in the sand, all of them replete from a meal of chicken, potato salad and thick slices of chocolate cake. There had been no attempt at conversation, merely a gentle silence. When Caleb became tired, they'd cleared the remains of their meal and headed home.

Delaney glanced up at Jake as he stepped back into the hall, empty-handed.

He was already looking at her.

The silence of the evening slipped between them, reminding them of all that had been said, all that had been implied.

All that still remained undone.

"Thank you for dinner," she murmured as he leaned one shoulder against the wall.

"Sure."

He hesitated, then said, "I'm sorry if I offended you by commenting on your...soberness."

The words took her off guard. "I—"

"I realize now I was being—"

"Honest." The word slipped from her lips unbidden. "You had a right to say what you felt."

"Not if it hurt you in the process."

She couldn't—*wouldn't*—admit that his comment had stung a little.

"I've been told I should guard my tongue. Unfortunately, I tend to say whatever's on my mind." He took a slow breath. "Therefore, I'm going to tell you this, as well. I only said what I said because I'm beginning to care what happens to you—whatever occurs over the custody situation with us and Caleb."

Her lips trembled, curving into a smile she could not contain. "Thank you."

His answering grin was warm and real and oh, so inviting. "Come on," he said, holding out his hand, "I'll walk you to your room."

His fingers were strong as they laced between her own. Though she felt a brief flutter of self-consciousness, Delaney fell into step beside him.

They came to a stop beside the door. The shadows of the hall hung cool and deep around them.

Jake didn't immediately step away. Instead, he turned to face her, so close that she had to tip her head back to meet his gaze. Surprisingly, he didn't speak, but then again, he didn't need to. It was all there in his eyes, his body. The wanting, the attraction. The barely submerged desire.

Her own pulse began to pound as he took a step forward. Thigh brushed against thigh, and she allowed him to plant his hands on the wall behind her.

"I'm going to kiss you, Delaney."

His voice was the barest of whispers. The sound was as delicate to her ears as the brush of a hummingbird's wing.

"I know."

His eyes focused on her mouth.

"Do you still think it's a mistake?"

"No."

"Do you think we should maintain our distance?"

"No." The whisper was far more telling than she had intended it to be.

"The last four nights, I've been longing for a kiss."

"Really?" The word escaped as a near-moan, a breathy sigh.

"Tonight I don't want to go to bed hungry."

Delaney shook her head.

Jake lifted one of his hands. With a single finger, he ran a tormenting trail from her temple, to her cheek, to her chin. She couldn't control the shiver that raced from that tiny point of contact.

"Do I frighten you?" he asked, his tone filled with a teasing indulgence.

Delaney found herself answering honestly. "Yes."

The seriousness of her features arrested his attention. The skimming finger halted its exploration for a moment and paused at the swell of her lower lip.

"Why?"

Her eyes skittered away, but with a slight nudge, he forced her to look at him.

"Because I don't know how to play your games," she finally whispered.

His eyes narrowed for a moment. "You think this is a game?"

She nodded.

His thumb rubbed against her lip. "No games, no tricks."

"Then what?"

"Honest emotion. The kind that nice people don't admit exist until they absolutely have to—passion. Even lust."

"I'm not sure I'm prepared to handle them, either."

He watched her with quiet eyes. "Why not?"

When she didn't speak, he took a step closer, until he stood so near to her the warmth of his body seemed to beckon an answering flood of heat in her own.

"What *are* you prepared to handle, Delaney?"

She fought to breathe. "A simple relationship. Mutual trust. An honest sharing of emotions."

"We've already crossed that line."

She took a shuddering gulp of air. "Not yet."

His head dipped, slowly, tormentingly. "Yes. We have," he whispered, just before his lips took her own.

Slow and hot.

If she were asked how to describe the kiss, she would remember it later as being slow and hot. His mouth moved across hers with a masculine assurance that she could only begin to delve. He asked nothing she wasn't prepared to give. There was no rush, no pressure for her to respond. Instead, he seemed content to explore. Then, he drew away.

With an exquisite reluctance, Delaney willed her fingers to curl into fists.

Her eyes flickered open. His brown eyes met hers with such a tangle of awareness and masculine expectancy that Delaney could scarcely believe the emotions had come from kissing her. Her!

She uncurled her fingers and reached to hesitantly touch his ribs.

He smiled and took an infinitesimal step forward.

She responded with an answering smile before her hands dug more firmly around the hard contours of his waist. She had only a fleeting impression of the strength beneath her palms before he bent to kiss her again.

This time, there was no reticence on his part or hers. What had started so simply became suddenly hungry and intense. He leaned into her, hip against hip, torso against torso. The warmth of the evening couldn't compete with the heat that was generated between them. An electric, breathless heat.

From outside, a honking horn and the hooting calls of a pair of passing teenagers jerked them back to their surroundings. Delaney cringed in embarrassment when she realized their silhouettes could be clearly seen through the French window as the kids careered around the corner.

Jake cupped her shoulders gently in his hands.

"Don't be embarrassed," he murmured. "What we're doing is natural, pleasurable."

She could only groan.

He chuckled, opening her door. "I'll see you in the morning." Leaning down, he tried to see her expression more clearly, wondering if the intensity of their kiss would frighten her away.

But when she glanced up at him, her eyes wide, the russet braid deliciously mussed, it wasn't the familiar nervousness he saw in her eyes. It was a velvet anticipation.

"Sweet dreams, Jake."

He grinned and planted a quick kiss on her lips. "You too."

Then he backed away and watched with an obscene amount of self-satisfaction as Delaney absentmindedly bumped her way through the doorway into her bedroom.

As the quiet of the house settled around him, Jake fought to still the misgivings he felt. He was playing with fire; he knew that. One day—one day soon—the decision about who would become Caleb's guardian would be made. There would be no winners in the situation. If Caleb was given to him, Delaney might later think he'd come to work for her with some sort of ulterior motive.

He sighed, realizing that he couldn't defend himself. He *had* agreed to help in the hopes of putting a wrench in the works. But from the moment he began his silent campaign to loosen this woman's reserve, he'd unconsciously sabotaged his own plans. He'd delved into the unknown. He'd dropped his distant attitude. He'd dressed this woman in his own clothes and spent a night absorbing the waves of warmth he'd endured each time he looked at her. He'd allowed her into his workshop—something he'd allowed no woman to ever do—and all the time she was admiring the strength of the medieval armor she saw, he'd been plotting to discover more chinks in the emotional armor she wore around her heart.

Then he'd kissed her.

There was no going back. Each day he was becoming a little more intrigued by this woman. A little more aroused. A little less distant. He could try to convince himself that it was done out of his love for Caleb, in case this woman should become his mother, out of his own sense of fairness, or even out of his own guilt.

But the truth of the matter was, this woman was burrowing her way under his skin, becoming lodged there. So much so that he didn't really know what he should do next.

But as the sliver of light disappeared from under her door, he couldn't deny that he had an indescribable yearning to be with her again tomorrow morning.

As well as the morning after that.

And the morning after that.

Chapter Nine

Jake weaved his way easily through the noontime crush at Sak's, heading for the escalators, which would take him up to the children's department, where he was supposed to meet Delaney. That morning, she'd discovered that Caleb had outgrown much of the wardrobe packed in his dresser drawers and plainly filled with a sense of purpose, she'd asked if Jake would bring the boy here during her lunch hour.

The whole idea pleased Jake more than it should. Marlene had never bothered to pick out clothes for Caleb. Instead, she'd made arrangements for charge accounts at a dozen stores and instructed Jake to "buy the boy whatever he needed, whenever he needed it."

Delaney, on the other hand, had begun making lists the moment she saw the situation. He had no doubt that the shopping spree would last far longer than an hour, and would involve purchasing a good deal more than new underwear and a few pairs of pants.

"Oys!" Caleb gestured toward a pretty mannequin dressed in a silk-and-lace teddy, and Jake had to chuckle.

"Not yet, Caleb. Give yourself a few years. Then remember that it's the clothing you'll refer to as 'toys,' and never the woman inside."

Caleb's head tilted, and his eyes took on a quizzical gleam. It wouldn't be long, Jacob realized, before the lad wouldn't need an explanation. He was growing so fast.

He stopped in his tracks as a realization struck him. What if he wasn't here to see the transformation? What if it was Delaney who led him through his adolescence?

A stab of very real pain shot through his chest, but he pushed it aside. As much as he hated the idea, he also had to be honest with himself. He'd seen a change come over Delaney McBride. He'd seen the hard-faced, dourly dressed research scientist soften into a giving, loving woman.

A mother.

She loved Caleb. Of that, Jake had no doubts. She would be desolate without the boy—even if she wouldn't admit it to herself yet.

But could Jake give him up? Could he say goodbye once and for all? Especially when his last memories of Caleb would be bound irretrievably to Delaney, as well?

Then it struck him. This sudden rush of anxiety wasn't about Caleb. Not really. It was about Delaney. About being forced to say goodbye to *her*.

About leaving her with only half of her transformation complete.

"Come on, Caleb. We've got a toy to buy for Delaney."

Caleb blinked at him in surprise, and Jake grinned, imagining Delaney's reaction when he slipped a package of his own into those she bought today. The little red camisole and the tap pants. Yes. They were intriguing, without being too off-putting for a woman like Delaney. The moment she saw them, she would blush, and her mind would be flooded with the thought that *he'd* bought them for her. That he'd even guessed her size correctly.

After all, he hadn't developed a reputation for being a bad boy for nothing. He knew his way around a lingerie department quite well. Quite well indeed.

"HOW IS EVERYTHING? Do you need some other sizes?"

Delaney jumped a little when the saleswoman's voice came to her from the other side of the dressing room door.

"No," she called out hurriedly. "Everything's fine. Just fine."

She waited until the woman moved on to another customer before looking at herself in the mirror again.

What in the world had got into her? What was she doing in the lingerie department of Sak's Fifth Avenue, trying on lingerie, for heaven's sake? And why, after she'd donned virginal white gowns, pink baby dolls and ivory peignoirs, was she thinking of buying this? *This?*

The black merry widow laced up the front, leaving a strip of bare skin between the cording. The cups were of lace, and the garment itself was of a shiny, thick satin. Below was a scrap of lace for panties, and garters that attached to lace-topped stockings.

It was wicked.

Utterly wicked.

And wonderful . . . a little voice sighed.

Delaney regretfully stroked the rich fabric, knowing she couldn't buy it. She wouldn't dare. If she wanted something daring, there was that red one. The tap pants and camisole she'd tried on earlier and sent back to the floor.

So why was it that inside her head there was a little imp of mischief that begged her to reconsider? Even if no one ever saw the merry widow but her, even if it gathered dust in her underwear drawer, even if it cost more than a small third-world country, why couldn't she indulge herself? Just this once?

Filled with determination, she quickly changed, gathered up her purse and the black ensemble and strode onto the main floor, making a beeline for the cash register.

"Laney!"

The cry of welcome made her stop in her tracks. Time became slow and sticky as she saw Caleb sitting on the counter, Jake holding out a pair of bills, a saleswoman folding a red silk camisole in tissue paper and sliding it into a bag, while a matching pair of tap pants made a crimson puddle on the glass surface at her side.

Then, just as slowly, she saw Jake's eyes drop to the items in her hand. The corset, the stockings, the panties.

A slow grin melted over his lips, drawing her forward against her will. When she was by his side, he bent to her ear, murmuring, "We seem to have had the same idea."

She didn't answer. She couldn't. Her heart was beating too madly, her throat had grown dry.

The saleswoman put his sack on the counter next to Caleb and began ringing up Delaney's purchases.

"Will you model it for me sometime?" he whispered, still so close he tickled the hairs by her ears.

"Which one?"

"Both."

She could only nod. Mutely.

His grin widened, and he touched her back, her waist, his fingers barely skimming the curve of her hips. Then he was picking Caleb up.

"Your sack, sir."

"It belongs to her," he said, nodding in Delaney's direction.

She could only blush, and it made him chuckle.

"I knew you'd do that," he said, touching her hot cheek as they turned and made their way to the escalators. "And I'm so glad you did."

THEY SPENT another two hours in the children's department, and finally left the store with a mountain of purchases piled in Jake's Jeep. Caleb, thoroughly worn out by the experience, sprawled in his car seat and promptly fell asleep, a red sucker he'd been given by the shoe salesman still clutched in his hand, half eaten.

"He's a mess," Delaney commented indulgently.

"He'll wash up."

A peaceful stillness settled between them, despite the echoing clatter of cars driving over metal grates, distant honks, and chattering shoppers.

"Can you drop me off at the institute?"

"Sure." Jake's brow furrowed. "Where's your Jag?"

She shrugged, not about to tell him that the car salesman she'd spoken with was looking it over in preparation for giving her a bid for a trade-in.

"I took a cab."

He didn't ask for a more detailed explanation, and she was glad of that.

Less than twenty minutes passed before the Jeep pulled to a stop at the main doors of the institute. Climbing from the front seat, Delaney surreptitiously gathered a few of the shopping bags and prepared to leave.

"Are any of those from the lingerie department?" Jake asked silkily.

She felt an all-too-familiar heat stain her cheeks. One that rose whenever she thought of their encounter at Sak's.

"No."

"Pity."

Delaney took one step back, then said, "Don't forget, my mother will be coming by at four to pick Caleb up for an outing."

"I won't. He'll be bathed, rested, and decked out in new clothes."

She couldn't help smiling herself. Quite giddily, in fact. It was so unlike her.

"Good. Are we still going to the library tonight?"

His brows waggled. "Unless you've got other plans."

"No," she said firmly. "I don't."

"Then I'll see you at six."

She bent to kiss Caleb on the nose, grimacing when the kiss was somewhat sticky. Stroking the little boy's hair, she allowed herself one indulgent smile. "Get a picture of him before you unstrap him. There's a pile of those little cameras in a box on the living room shelf."

"I know, I know."

Then she was looking at Jake. Big, strong, lovable Jake.

"Bye."

He saluted and put the car in gear, driving away.

Leaving her with the thought that maybe, just maybe, she *should* have brought the lingerie packages with her after all.

A BLAST OF SUMMER HEAT hit Delaney full in the face as she and Linda stepped through the etched-glass doors of the Lexington Institute a few hours later. But the breath-robbing sensation was nothing compared to the punch to her gut that she felt when she saw a cherry-red Jeep parked in the loading zone.

She looked for Jake immediately. She couldn't help the action—even as she damned herself for such foolishness. When she found him leaning against the passenger-side door, his legs propped in front of him, one ankle crossed lazily over the other, she forgot all else in favor of far more tantalizing indulgences.

"The man has come to fetch you?"

"Um-hmm..."

"Trouble with the Jaguar?"

"Nooo..." Delaney said, hedging.

"I see," Linda drawled.

"I doubt it. His coming for me is a practical gesture—purely innocent, I assure you."

"It can't be. Not with a man like that—someone who's the epitome of a 'bad boy.' No one on earth has a right to look like that. Not and show up here at the stuffy capital of the world."

"Now, Linda...since Caleb is spending the afternoon with my mother, Jake is merely here to take me to the Rutger Branch Library. He wants me to check out some child-psychology books he's found helpful. Then we're going to select some picture books for Caleb. According to Jake, reading time is very important, especially at Caleb's age.''

"I just might need a book," Linda offered.

"Don't you dare!"

Linda shot her a teasing glance. "Soon, dear, I will demand an introduction—as well as an evening alone with you for a debriefing. We'll call it a late birthday celebration, if you like.''

"My birthday has passed."

"But you and I haven't had an official party yet. No one has. Did you know that the institute wanted to hold some awful cocktail affair in your honor?''

Delaney looked at Linda in dismay, realizing that if such an event occurred, she would be required to bring a date. She could just imagine what the board of directors would say if she brought Jake—or what Jake would say if she asked him to go.

Her lack of enthusiasm must have been plainly written on her face, because Linda laughed. "Don't worry. They put me in charge of the festivities." Her eyes twinkled. "I wouldn't be so cruel as to force a confrontation between you, your employers, and your…nanny. I've already planned something more intimate, more meaningful.''

Delaney felt a twinge of foreboding, wondering what the mischievous Linda had planned, but before she could ask, Linda laughed and waggled a finger in Delaney's direction.

"Enjoy your time with Jake—it's bound to be filled with surprises. After all, the change in wardrobe should cause enough of a shock for one evening."

Chuckling, Linda moved toward her own car, leaving Delaney isolated and feeling just a little awkward. That afternoon, Linda had caught Delaney sneaking into her office with the set of shopping bags. When she emerged wearing a newly bought set of jeans, sandals, a cotton shirt and a boxy linen jacket, Linda had been hard-pressed to contain her delight.

Delaney was having a far more difficult time adjusting to her clothes. Although she was modestly dressed, there was something about the casual attire that made her feel...conspicuous. More...sensual. Attainable.

Her eyes skipped to the Jeep and the man who waited there. Since he was partially screened by the hedge bordering the walk, he hadn't seen her yet, and she was glad. It gave her a minute to gather her breath. Her confidence.

The ploy didn't work as well as she had hoped. Instead, she found herself watching Jake with an intensity that bordered on fascination. He was beautiful. There was no other way to describe him. The hot sun beat down upon his dark head, caressing the waves drawn back from his face and secured at his nape. His shoulders were broad and well-defined within the soft fabric of the T-shirt he wore. The jeans that encased his hips and legs should have been declared illegal for what they did to a woman, worn nearly white-blue at the knees, the thighs, the fly.

Delaney wrenched her eyes and her thoughts away, wondering what had come over her lately. She wasn't normally so crass. So...

Needy.

He looked up, seeing her. For the life of her, she couldn't move, couldn't think. Stretching with a slow, catlike grace, he stood and walked forward, taking the sunglasses from his eyes so that she could not mistake the fact that he, too, had sensed the electricity between them.

Tonight they would be together for a few hours.

Alone.

"Hi."

How could he make such a simple word so silky, so intimate?

"Hello." She felt a moment of self-consciousness, wondering what he would say next, what *she* would say next.

Before she knew what was about to occur, he took her face in his hands, studying her features. Then he bent to place a soft kiss upon her lips.

In an instant, Delaney knew she was in trouble. The gesture was completely innocent and therefore even more appealing, rocking her to her very foundation because she wanted more, so much more.

"Thank you, Delaney."

His husky comment caused a shiver to course down her spine.

"For what?"

"The nice digs, a chance to spend a little more time with Caleb. I just realized that I haven't bothered to thank you until today."

A tremulous smile tugged at her lips, and she tried to tamp it down. She shouldn't feel so pleased. But she did. When she arranged for the honeymoon house, she'd purposely given Jake the corner room. One that let the sunshine flood in each morning and had a marvelous view of the garden in the backyard.

"You're welcome."

"I had the windows open last night."

"Oh?"

"I thought I could hear music." His lips twitched in a smile. "Perhaps even a little humming?"

She blushed. She hadn't realized that he could hear her. She'd thought that any noise she made had been under her breath. But then, she'd forgotten how any noise traveled in the little house they lived in—especially with the windows left open to catch the breezes.

"You've been listening to those Muppet tapes, haven't you?"

"Guilty," she confessed, flustered. "That song about it ain't easy being green gets to me every time."

"You certainly lulled me to sleep."

Implying that he must have listened to her while he was lying in bed. Encased in darkness. Wearing . . . a sheet? Nothing at all? The thought caused her knees to tremble.

"It was almost like having my own little lullaby."

What could she say to that? Should she try to say anything? She might be the only person involved in this conversation who read any double entendres into the replies. But, judging by the brown-black glimmer in his eyes, she doubted it.

"Would you be willing to perform another chorus at some later date?"

"I suppose," she answered hesitantly.

His smile was warm and genuine. "Good. I'll look forward to it." His fingers trailed down her arm to her elbow. "Listen, I didn't have a chance to call you today to relay a change in plans."

"That's fine. I understand your schedule."

"I know we agreed to go to the library for a few hours, but I wondered if you were free the rest of this evening, as well? I thought we could make our trip to the library, then I'll take you to dinner."

"What about Caleb?"

"My brother Nick offered to meet your mother and take Caleb to the local McDonald's Playland. He's trying to show his latest girlfriend that he's the sensitive type."

"Well . . ."

"Relax. Nick has served as a baby-sitter many times before. He honestly likes the kid, and their outings are a regular event. Wouldn't you like a night away for a change?"

"Yes," she responded easily. "Yes, I would."

Nodding in approval, he took her briefcase. Placing his hand in the hollow of her back, he steered her toward the Jeep. At the passenger door, he set her case behind the seat, then waited for her to climb inside.

After settling into the driver's seat, he thrummed the engine into action and roared out of the parking lot, causing more than one head to turn and watch them pass. Delaney could only wonder at the gossip that would be running rampant at the institute by the following morning. She had a reputation at Lexington for being a loner, a woman who devoted her time to her work and little else—certainly never indulging in any sort of a social life. To be seen cruising out of the complex with someone of Jake Turk's overwhelmingly good looks would cause a rash of titillating gossip.

So why was the thought so exciting?

He drove in silence for a few minutes, but when he kept casting glances her way, she asked, "Is something wrong?"

"I like what you're wearing."

She shifted uncomfortably, wondering if she'd been too obvious in changing her wardrobe. Did the jeans look too new? The shirt too well pressed? The shoes too clean?

"Thank you."

"Was that what you had squirreled away in those shopping bags?"

"Yes. I got them before..."

"Our trip to the lingerie department."

She could feel herself flushing.

Damn.

He jerked his attention away, returning his scrutiny to the road, but after a few minutes, he was looking at her again.

"Do you always wear your hair like that?"

Her hands immediately flew to the simple twist at the back of her head. She didn't need a mirror to tell her that the wind had played havoc with the style, tugging it free of its moorings.

"There's nothing wrong with it," Jake hastened to assure her. "It's just that it's a little...formal with jeans."

"I didn't have time to do anything else with it."

The Jeep rolled to a stop in the parking lot of the library.

Jake grinned at her and reached to touch her chin. "Don't look so solemn. One hour. Only one hour of books. Then I promise I'll take you to dinner."

But as he led her to the doors, it wasn't the time in the library she was worried about. Her encounters with Jacob Turk were causing her to look more closely at the woman she had become, and the woman she was destined to be if events continued along their same path. To her horror, she was learning that such inner examinations were proving to be far more discouraging than encouraging. She didn't want to be the type of woman who lived only for her work, who had no family, no real friends, no real personal joys in which to indulge a little bit of her time. More than that, she didn't want to raise a young boy in such an environment.

She thought of the coin Jake had given her, with its image of a castle. She'd put it on the windowsill next to her bed.

A hand seemed to clench around her chest. Jake had been right. She didn't know how to enjoy herself. Just acknowledging the fact wasn't enough. Something more had to be done.

Her fingers trembled, and she curled them into fists. Change frightened her. It had always frightened her. Perhaps her childhood was responsible. Her parents had moved her from school to school, trying to offer her the best in educational opportunities. Just when she became accustomed to a situation, she was withdrawn and thrown into another class, another life-style. She'd sworn that once she'd established her own home and settled into a challenging career, such rude awakenings would never occur again.

She'd been wrong. A fresh tide of change seemed to be rearing up in front of her. She could only pray she had the courage to face it—or the strength to live with the consequences if she didn't.

Because, for the first time, she consciously admitted that she *wanted* to be Caleb's mother. She *wanted* him to be a part of her life. She *wanted* him to be her child.

Just as much as she wanted Jacob Turk to be so much more than the boy's nanny.

THE NEXT HOUR passed in muted whispers as Jake helped her check out the texts he wanted her to study, then took her on a tour of the children's wing of the library. There were no lingering glances, no exchanges of banter, no conversation containing any sort of sexual overtones.

Delaney didn't know how such an overpoweringly businesslike attitude had begun to infuse the evening. Maybe it was the hushed atmosphere of the library, but she was inclined to believe that Jacob's commitment to her education was responsible for the change. His dedication and concentration were without equal. Delaney could only wish the same could be said about her.

Her eyes skipped to the line of his brow. A lock of hair spilled over his forehead, so long, so wavy, that she wanted to touch it, wanted to draw it back and smooth it into place.

Stop it! What was she thinking? This was a library! One filled with people intent upon research and personal development. She was supposed to be huddled over this table examining the effectiveness of a picture book, for heaven's sake!

Her inner castigation had no effect. She couldn't tear her gaze from Jacob Turk. What was even more disturbing was that she was beginning to enjoy the tingling sensations such long glances inspired.

"Is something wrong?"

Delaney jerked, then felt a warmth rise into her cheeks when she realized that she'd been caught in her musings. Glancing down at the brightly illustrated book, she busied herself with flipping through the pages. "No."

"You looked suddenly... wistful."

She compulsively locked her gaze with his. "Did I?" The words escaped before she could prevent them.

"Wistful, and a little agitated."

"Oh."

Several beats of silence followed her inane response. The quiet fairly pulsed with discomfort. Without warning, the tomblike atmosphere of the Rutger Branch Library didn't seem quite so peaceful.

"Are you hungry?" He reached across the table to still her fingers, which had unconsciously begun toying with the pages again.

She could only nod.

"Good. Let's call it a night and get something to eat. Are you in the mood for anything particular?"

She cleared her throat, a tingling settling low in the pit of her belly at the contact of his hand. His thumb shifted, moving to stroke across the ridge of her knuckles. And she suddenly needed more. So much more.

"No, I—"

"Delaney McBride?"

The query came from a point over her shoulder. In seconds, the mood between her and Jake shattered as his attention was drawn away. When his eyes widened in disbelief, she took a quick glance of her own.

"Oh, no." The words popped unbidden from her mouth upon her first sight of a six-foot gorilla holding a dozen balloons and a gaily wrapped present. The ape placed the package on the table in front of her and thrust the balloons into her hands.

"Many happy returns from Linda and your colleagues at the Lexington Institute!" Taking a pitch pipe from the paisley vest he wore over his ridiculously furry suit, he blew one note, alerting at least a half-dozen people intent upon reading. When the gangly ape began to sing, Delaney covered her face with her hands and fought a scalding tide of embarrassment. She should have taken Linda's open curiosity as a warning. She should have kept the location of her meeting with Jake secret.

After blowing one more note, the oversize monkey began to sing. "We missed you on your birthday, we hope we're not too late, to wish you lots of happiness, and send along this cake. We would've hired a stripper, but since you're now so old, we sent a furry fellow, in the hopes it's not too bold. Ya-da, ya-da, ya-da..."

"Shh!" A matronly woman in support hose with a sweater slung over her shoulders dodged from behind the circulation desk and marched toward them. "You must be quiet!"

The ape paid little attention, launching into a rendition of a soft-shoe routine while the library patrons reacted by either laughing or pointing in their direction.

Looking pleadingly at Jake, Delaney was relieved immeasurably when he quickly gathered their belongings, tucked the pastry box under one arm, grabbed her wrist with the other and dragged her outside.

The ape, after a moment of indecision, followed, still dancing, so Jake gestured toward his Jeep, at the far end of the parking lot. Racing toward it, they climbed inside, and within moments they were roaring down the street.

Delaney didn't even bother to look and see where they were going. They had escaped—that was all that mattered.

"Why didn't you tell me it was your birthday?"

"What?" She lowered her hands to stare at him.

"Your birthday. Why didn't you tell me tonight was your birthday?"

She gripped the cake box when the Jeep hit a dip, and the dessert threatened to slide onto the floor. "It was weeks ago. Linda was asked by the institute to organize some sort of celebration. I guess this was her idea."

"Linda?"

"My sec—one of my friends at work."

His brow creased. "Let me guess. Your birthday was the night I invited you to meet me at Twin Towers. You were originally going somewhere with a friend, weren't you? Why didn't you tell me?''

She shrugged, not wanting him to think that his request to join him at the amusement park had served to inconvenience her. "We didn't really have anything special planned."

He reached across the space between the seats to take her hand. "I guess it's up to me to make it up to you for not being able to celebrate on the official day. Tonight, you and I will make this a birthday to re-member—even if it is a bit late. Deal?''

Looking into those eyes, those chocolate-colored eyes . . . how could she refuse?

Chapter Ten

Delaney didn't know what she'd expected, but she certainly hadn't anticipated being driven into the heart of Los Angeles to a little restaurant carved out of a brick wall. A neon sign blinked crazily overhead, flashing out the legend *Adam's Ribs* for all the world to see.

"Do you like barbecue?" Jake asked after maneuvering into a narrow parallel parking place.

"I . . . think so."

His brow lifted in confusion at her odd reply.

"I've never had them before."

"Never had them?" It was obvious that the idea was inconceivable to him.

"When I was little, my mother was a health nut— you know the type. Bulgur and tofu and soy burgers."

She caught his very visible shudder.

"What an awful thing to do to a kid." He swung from the Jeep and rounded the hood. "Sounds to me like you're overdue for a dose of red meat and cholesterol. Mind you, I don't indulge that often myself, but birthdays demand a little latitude.'' He gestured toward her linen jacket. "You might want to leave that here. Barbecue sauce tends to splatter, and it will be hot inside.''

"Okay.''

To her own amazement, she felt a very real reluctance to remove that simple covering. The cotton of her blouse was soft and slightly sheer, riding the swells of her breasts and revealing just a hint of the lace of her plain white camisole beneath. But maybe he wouldn't notice.

He noticed. In an instant, she knew he'd seen each detail of her attire. Judging by the dark flicker deep in his eyes, he didn't disapprove.

The weight of his palm against her back felt better than it should as they hurried across the street and into Adam's Ribs. Upon stepping through the door, they were met with a blast of music from a battered jukebox in the corner, the smell of roasting meat and the din of at least eighty people competing to be heard.

"Pretty great, huh?''

"What?''

Jake bent close, so close that his words tickled the hairs above her ear. "It's a pretty great place. You'll love it, I promise.''

A waitress dressed in denim shorts and a chambray shirt led them toward a booth in the back and handed them a menu written on a miniature blackboard.

"Anything to drink?"

"Two beers."

Delaney opened her mouth to refuse, then inwardly shrugged. Why not? She'd never tasted it, but that didn't mean she couldn't tonight.

Jake leaned across the booth. "I'd recommend the—"

He was drowned out by a burst of drums from the jukebox.

"What?"

Grimacing, he slid from the booth and moved to sit beside her. Instantly she became aware of the strength of his thighs, the warmth of his body.

"I'd recommend the sample platter, since it's your first time here."

She nodded. "Whatever you say."

When the waitress returned with their drinks, Jake gave the woman their orders. Then they were alone. As alone as two people could be in a crowded room filled with laughing and chattering people.

"If your mother was such a health nut, you must have had interesting birthday parties as a youngster."

She took a sniff of her beer, wrinkling her nose at the smell. One taste and she realized she was in trouble. She'd never had much of a head for alcohol, and even less affection for the taste. The yeasty, fermented drink definitely didn't make the list of her favorites.

"Something wrong?"

Jake must have caught her reaction. She hoped he couldn't see the slight flush of embarrassment slipping into her cheeks.

"No. Thanks."

"Did you want a different brand?"

"No. It's fine." When he continued to look at her intently, she finally offered, "I just don't drink the stuff very often."

His lips twitched in a wry smile. "You should have said something. You don't have to drink it just to please me." There was a pause filled with the pulsing beat of music, a throbbing that was beginning to seep into her bones.

His hand stole out to clasp her own, twining their fingers together. "Do you mind if my attention is completely…personal this evening? And we leave all talk of Caleb at the door?"

"No." She was sure he never heard her answer in the noisy restaurant, but he must have read her lips, because his eyes became hot and intimate. She wanted to look away, but his gaze held her fast.

The music faded into a strange sort of silence, and he adjusted the tone of his voice accordingly. The husky murmur he adopted slid down her spine in a searing caress.

"There's something building between us, Delaney. Something that I don't think is going to go away.

It feels suspiciously like desire, the raw, elemental kind that gnaws at your insides."

The sentiments, spoken aloud, had much more of an impact than she would ever have imagined.

He slid his thumb over the delicate bones of her wrist, causing her to shiver. It was a simple caress, but her reaction said so much.

"We might not like it, but it is happening. It's strong. Powerful. You feel it, too, Delaney. I know you do."

She couldn't deny it.

"Do you object?"

There it was, out in the open. If she said the idea made her uncomfortable, or that she had no desire to see him again, he would bow to her wishes. But if she agreed . . .

"Will you dance with me, Delaney?"

She hadn't even been aware there was a dance floor at Adam's Ribs, but she didn't care. When he slid from the booth and offered his hand, she took it, knowing she was tacitly agreeing to far more than a simple rumba or cha-cha.

She would probably be hurt. Jake had warned her far in advance that he didn't want a permanent relationship. She knew that, after Jake had rejected her, after her heart had been broken, she would look back at this moment and realize that she could have prevented each ounce of pain. She could have risen to her feet, turned her back, and walked out the door.

But at this point in time, she didn't care. She would rather regret the consequences of giving in to the moment, but she knew she would never live to regret giving Jake a chance.

He led her toward the far end of the room, his eyes leaving her face only when it was necessary to navigate the sea of tables. When he'd finally managed to secure a few feet of space, he pulled her into his arms.

From the moment his hands splayed across the gentle slope of her back, Jake knew he'd found his own corner of heaven. She felt good against him. Soft and lithe and womanly. She hesitated for an instant, as if unsure what to do, but when he began a simple two-step, she responded.

They didn't speak. They didn't need to. There were subtle emotions bubbling below the surface of the music and the sway of their bodies. An acceptance of all that had been said. A wild anticipation of where it would all lead.

Jake knew that things were rushing between them, that he should force his feelings for this woman aside. She wasn't his type—she was too cool, too sophisticated. She didn't belong in his world any more than he belonged in hers. And the situation with Caleb complicated matters even more.

But he was beginning to believe that something stronger than both of them had brought them together—fate, karma, it didn't really need a name. All that mattered was that whenever he touched Delaney McBride, he felt the need to protect her, possess her.

She had such a complicated personality. A strength and a shyness. Determination and vulnerability. She didn't fawn over his body or frown at his life-style. She merely accepted him as he was.

For now.

Until matters with Caleb would have to be decided. Until one of them was made guardian of a little boy and the other became an interloper.

Nearly a foot of space separated them, and he shifted his arms to the middle of her spine, needing her nearer. She didn't resist, though her eyes grew wide and wary. Beautiful hazel eyes, as large and clear as a doe's.

"I want to feel you next to me." The words couldn't possibly have carried over the boom of the music, but she must have interpreted them nonetheless, because she allowed her feet to settle between his own, her hands to rest upon his waist.

For a time, the proximity was enough. For a time. Then his vow to pace their intimacy a little more slowly snapped when her hands lifted, rubbed, then splayed wide over his chest.

The band began to rock, beating out a primeval rhythm, fast, strong. But their own movements became slower, more deliberate. Swinging her closer still, Jake pulled her hips against the cradle of his thighs. Her stomach rubbed intimately against him, making him wonder if she felt the response. A response that had been there for most of the evening.

Supporting her, he bent her body backward over his arm. The impromptu dip seemed to delight her, and he was glad. Wrapping her more tightly in his embrace, he began to lead her in an erotic sequence of dips and sways, one that made his heart begin to thunder and his skin to pepper in a rash of gooseflesh.

Did she have any idea how sensual she appeared? The softer clothing she wore was more of a turn-on than he would have imagined. In the flashing light of a red strobe, the cotton fabric of her blouse became all but transparent, revealing the lace of her camisole beneath. One of the buttons at her neck had come undone, displaying the faintest shadow of her cleavage, and Jake wondered what it would be like to place his mouth there. Just once. A tiny taste.

Unable to help himself, he dipped her again, pressing his lips to that spot, flicking his tongue out to briefly tease her. She gasped; he felt it. But when he drew back, she appeared far from offended. Her fingers lifted to tangle in his hair. Her eyes grew dark, her skin flushed.

Their dance soon adopted an even more intimate rhythm, and Jake began to wonder if he would be able to breathe, to think. No woman had ever made him feel this way. As if he were special.

"Let's get out of here."

"But—"

"We'll get the order to go."

Taking her wrist, he dragged her through the bumping, gyrating group that surrounded them. Locating their waitress, he whispered something in her ear and slipped her several bills. By the time they reached the front door, she appeared with a large brown bag and two paper cups. Handing the drinks to Delaney, Jake thanked the woman, then grabbed the sack and led Delaney into the darkness.

He took her to Hoover Park. After locating a battered quilt behind the Jeep's rear seat, he led her to a spot in the middle of the lawn.

She eyed the blanket suspiciously. "Do you do this a lot?"

He grinned, sensing that the absence of the music and of the innate protection of the crowd had brought back a bit of her reserve.

"No. I do a lot of moving. Yvette is building a new house, and being the oldest brother, I have somehow inherited the job of delivering the pieces of antique furniture she finds. Invariably I arrive at an out-of-the-way flea market to discover that she's bought a delicate Victorian piece with these little carved naked cherubs all over it. She then expects me to get it home without a scratch. Therefore, I have learned to be prepared."

He spread the blanket on the ground and gestured for her to sit. She complied, settling herself rather stiffly on her knees at first. Then, seeing the way he flung himself on his stomach, she relaxed a little, her back easing, her body shifting to the side. It wasn't much, but it was a definite sign of progress on his part if he could get her to relax her iron control at least that much. He didn't think he'd ever met a woman more formal, more strictly devoted to decorum.

Knowing he needed to set her at ease again, he tore open the sack and quickly loaded two plates with ribs, sliced French bread and coleslaw. He handed the first plate to Delaney, then one of the cups.

"Beer?"

He laughed when she couldn't seem to keep herself from wrinkling her nose.

"It's a diet soda. It seems to be the drink of choice for most people these days."

She took a sip, closing her eyes and sighing in delight. "Manna from heaven."

The park slumbered about them in moon-washed freshness as they ate their food. If not for the faint drip, drip, sound made by a rainbird some distance away, they would have spent the entire time in silence. A warm silence. A welcoming one.

Once they'd finished, Jake stuffed the remains of their meal into the sack and rose to put it in a distant oil drum used as a garbage can. When he returned, Delaney had stretched out on the blanket. Her shoes lay a few feet away in the grass. One hand rested on the flat plane of her stomach, while the other had been flung above her head.

He paused. She looked so unconsciously sexy, so seductive, lying on his blanket that way. As if she were waiting for him to join her. Kiss her.

"Tired?"

She shook her head, but did not open her eyes. "No. I was just thinking what a wonderful evening this has been."

"So I managed to make up for ruining your birthday?"

She lifted one eyelid ever so slightly, so that she could peer at him quite seriously. "You didn't ruin my birthday."

"I forced you to come to Twin Towers."

"I came willingly."

"I made you sit through one of my shows."

Her lips twitched in a coy smile. "I enjoyed it. Imagine—I have become privy to the backstage secrets of Tar the Barbarian."

He grimaced. "It can get pretty hectic around show time."

"Do you enjoy it?"

He shrugged. "In a way. But I want more."

More.

Delaney studied him quite thoroughly when he echoed the thought that she herself had entertained not so long ago.

"What do you want, Jacob Turk?" she asked softly.

His eyes were nearly hidden in shadow, but she knew they were trained upon her.

"Which answer do you prefer to hear? The one I feed the press, or the real one?"

"The real one."

He shifted, staring out into the shadows for some time—so long, she wondered if he wasn't going to answer her. Then he said, "I want to wake up in the morning, knowing I've made a difference. I want to know I've met my challenges head-on."

He became so quiet, so still, that she found she couldn't move, could barely breathe. A tightness gripped her throat, so touched was she by his answer. He had to be a strong person indeed to admit such a thing to her, someone he'd known only a short while.

When he propped himself on his arms above her, she did not demur. Indeed, she met him halfway. The desire that had smoldered on the dance floor erupted full-force. Soon it wasn't enough to merely kiss, touch.

Taking his shoulders, she drew him over her body. As their tongues met, clashed, she willingly surrendered to his weight, hard muscle and bone, pressing into her womanly softness. Moaning, she reveled in the feelings, the exquisite feelings. Her hands trailed over his shoulders, his waist, his buttocks.

The park disappeared around them, leaving only a storm of passion, a symphony of need. When he slid his palm between them to cup her breast, she arched, needing the exhilaration, the fire. His mouth took hers hungrily, showing that the same emotions thundered through him. When he slipped his leg between hers to press against the part of her that ached, she moaned, her eyes opening wide.

He lay above her, his face in shadow, his eyes dark and molten. Bit by bit, as they both strove to catch their breath and gain some control over all that had occurred, the noises of the park returned. The drip, drip, of the rainbird, the sigh of the grass, the rustling of the trees.

"You've made me crave such encounters." She was the first to speak, and that fact surprised her. Mere hours ago, she wouldn't have had the courage to speak to him so honestly about her feelings.

"I don't want to rush you."

Her fingers touched his cheek. "Thank you."

"But I do want to know if I'm wasting my time."

The darkness grew thick with a thousand unanswered questions about the future. But Delaney found the uncertainty to be of little consequence when measured against the moment.

"No. You're not wasting your time."

He smiled. That quick, boyish grin that never ceased to warm her heart. "Happy birthday, Delaney."

Delaney closed her eyes and wrapped her arms around his shoulders, knowing this evening would never be forgotten, could never be dismissed.

Chapter Eleven

Within moments, Jake and Delaney had thrown away the empty containers, gathered up the quilt and climbed into the Jeep. Through it all, Jake had used every opportunity to touch her hand, her face, her hair, until they were seated side by side and he wove their fingers together.

Delaney knew it was a tacit announcement, that he was drawn to her, that he wanted her, and that he would not be leaving her at the door to her bedroom. She supposed the entire situation should have shocked her, given her solitary life-style up to now, but it didn't. No, she wished away the miles, prayed that Nick would be keeping Caleb for a few more hours. She wanted this evening. She wanted the lovemaking that would surely follow. She wanted to know what it would be like to be held by a man of Jake's grace and power.

She wanted *him*.

But it wasn't to be. She knew that the moment they turned the corner leading to the honeymoon house and saw the simple sedan parked at her curb.

"Nick is here." She sighed, impatient at the delay.

"That isn't Nick's car."

As soon as the words were uttered, a shape emerged from the driver's seat. A very tall, imposing middle-aged woman with oversize glasses and a severe suit.

"It's Marlene's lawyer," Jake said, even as Delaney guessed who it must be.

She immediately became frantic, combing at her hair with her fingers, trying to brush out the pieces of grass. "Were the toys picked up? Did I remember to move the laundry off the couch? What about Caleb, will it look bad that he's not here?"

"Calm down, Delaney. Everything will be fine."

But Delaney wasn't so sure. Especially when they pulled to a stop and the waiting woman glanced at her watch and sighed.

"Ms. McBride?" she asked, in one of those schoolmarmish sorts of voices that never ceased to put Delaney on the defensive.

"Yes, ma'am. I'm Delaney McBride."

The woman sniffed in disapproval, her glance darting from the wildness of Delaney's hair to her rumpled clothing.

"I am Twila Atkinson. Marlene Detry's lawyer."

Delaney held out her hand in greeting, then, seeing a smear of barbecue sauce, drew it back again.

"I believe you were aware that I would be dropping by now and again to check on Caleb."

"Yes, but I thought you'd call first."

The woman's stare was hard. "Obviously." Her gaze bounced in Jake's direction. "Mr. Turk, is there a reason for your being here?"

Jake seemed to be the only person still at ease. He leaned against the Jeep, one hand tucked into his pocket. "There was a mix-up with my contract. Marlene forgot to cancel it. Ms. McBride and I agreed that I should stay until the first week of July."

"Mmm-hmm..." The woman's response was such that Delaney knew she'd made a mental note to check with the agency for confirmation. "Where's the boy?"

Delaney glanced in supplication at Jake, who made the necessary response. "My brother took him to McDonald's."

"Mmm." Again she glanced at her watch. "Very well. I will return for another visit later this week. Good evening, Ms. McBride."

Delaney stood frozen until the woman's car disappeared into the darkness. "She hates me."

Jake laughed.

"No! I could tell! She hates me. She thinks that Caleb should have been here. With me. That I should have been baking him cookies or... or reading him stories."

"Every mother needs and deserves a break from her children now and again."

"But *she* doesn't think so," Delaney said, waving a hand in the direction the car had taken. "What am I going to do?" she asked weakly, then turned and ran to the house. Letting herself in, she threw open the door, seeing it as the lawyer would have seen it, the living room with a few toys scattered on the floor, the laundry folded on the couch, the empty juice glass on the coffee table, the Muppet tapes strewn on a shelf.

Immediately she began to clean, moving with a frantic energy that even she couldn't have explained. All she knew was that she had to fix things. She had to fix them before Twila Atkinson returned for her next visit.

"Delaney!" Jake caught her arm, forcing her to stop.

"No. No, don't you see? I've got to get ready. Everything has to be perfect. I can't let her take him away." Her throat became tight, dry. "I can't..."

Jake couldn't ignore her panic, or the entreaty he found in her eyes. As much as it pained him to do so, he pulled her close, whispering, "You've only had him a few weeks. Surely—"

"But he's *mine!* He's my little boy. I know I've only known him a short time, but...but don't you see? I wake up each morning thinking how I'll spend my time with him. I worry about him twenty-four hours a day, and pray that somehow, some way, he'll come to accept me in his life.''

A glimmer of moisture appeared at the edge of her lashes.

''Is that so much different from a woman who has carried her baby inside her for nine months?''

Whirling, she ran to her bedroom.

As the door slammed behind her, Jake sighed, rubbing at his chest, which had suddenly become too tight and too heavy.

What was he going to do?

THE NEXT MORNING, he emerged from his bedroom to discover that Caleb had already been bathed, dressed and fed. When he asked why Delaney had let him sleep, he discovered that she'd taken three weeks' vacation from work and she intended to do everything possible to show Ms. Atkinson that she meant business.

And so she did. The next time the lawyer appeared for one of her surprise visits, it was to discover that the house was spotless, Caleb was dressed in freshly ironed overalls and the smell of baking bread permeated the air—Delaney had been keeping loaves of bread dough purchased from a nearby bakery rising on the counter every day, just to ensure that particular detail.

It would have been amusing, if Jake hadn't found himself so torn by the proceedings. He was beginning to see the way she doted on the child—as well as the way Caleb responded to her. Just as Jake had surmised earlier, there was something about Delaney's nature that fed the boy's soul. All the tenderness and motherly indulgence that Marlene had never seen fit to give him.

What would she do if Caleb was taken from her when she was just beginning to trust herself, to allow herself to care? But on the other hand, what would Jake do if *he* never had a chance to develop his own relationship with the boy?

Added to that was the fact that Jake was also drawn to Delaney in very different ways. If things weren't so impossible between them, he might even consider the idea that the feelings they shared could be something binding. Real. If it weren't for the job back east threatening the time that remained, or the way the custody issue hadn't been resolved yet...

If.

Hadn't he learned the uselessness of such a word?

"I've got to stop in at the lab for a few minutes today," Delaney said, entering the basement, Caleb on her hip. He was fingering her hair, mussing it no end, and causing them both to giggle.

"My mother wants to take Caleb to the studio and out to dinner afterward."

"He'll like that." Jake continued to sweep the floor, hoping that she wouldn't see he'd lost his train of thought and wasn't really absorbing what she said.

"How long will it take to move all the exercise equipment down here?"

"Only a couple of hours."

Delaney looked pensive. "Are you sure you want to give it to me? It must be frightfully expensive. You'll probably want it later."

"It would cost too much to send it back east."

Once again, that unspoken threat of time hung over their heads.

"Tell you what…go make your stop at the lab. I'll watch Caleb until your mother comes. Then, when you come back, I'll take you through all this stuff and show you how it works."

"Great." She chucked Caleb under the chin. "Will you be a good boy today?"

He nodded.

"I'll see you tonight, then."

She put him down on the floor—and for the first time since Caleb had been left in her care, his little chin wobbled and his hands reached out as if to grasp her. Something that sounded very much like "Mama" emerged from his lips.

Delaney stood motionless, stunned, then hauled him close in a quick hug.

Leaving Jake to feel like a heel. An absolute heel.

"HERE, Linda. These are those files Burt needs. I'll stop by at the end of the week again to make sure everything is okay. Otherwise, I'm on vacation."

"Great! You deserve it. No one complained about taking a few extra hours of work. Considering you haven't taken a vacation since you arrived here, they were glad to do it.''

Delaney slipped a hand into her pocket. "There's one more thing I hoped you could do for me." She took out a sheet of information regarding the house in Beverly Hills. "I wondered if you knew of a reputable Realtor."

Linda, who had bent over the ledger spread out on the counter again, glanced up in surprise. "What for?"

"I'm thinking of selling the house."

Her expression remained blank. "Are you serious?"

"Yes. I called my parents the other night and made an offer on the honeymoon house. They wanted to just give it to me, but I've finally convinced them to accept a fair price. Caleb really seems to like it there, and..."

Linda was already reaching for the phone. "I'll see what I can do." But her voice was incredulous. "You really want to sell that place?"

"It's a mausoleum."

"That fact never seemed to bother you before."

Delaney grinned, causing Linda's brows to raise even more. Suddenly Delaney realized that the grin was not a reaction that Linda was accustomed to seeing from her.

"Let me know if you turn anything up."

"Does Jake know about that house?"

Only then did Delaney pause. "No."

"I see."

Delaney hesitated in the act of turning toward her office. "I didn't think it necessary to tell him."

"And just what else haven't you told him, other than where you really live? Does he know what you do here at the institute? Just how many degrees you hold?"

"Details, Linda." But Delaney couldn't deny the niggling guilt she felt as she closed herself in the bathroom next to her office and changed into the exercise gear she'd brought to work, as well as a well-worn tank top that belonged to Jake. She then slid into a pair of aerobic shoes and her jeans. The denims were getting softer, becoming well-worn. It was a feeling she liked, offering her something akin to a sense of accomplishment. She'd come a long way since meeting Jake Turk. If she took her time about confronting the rest of her fears head-on, who could blame her?

When she emerged again, Linda's brows arched at the change of clothing. "I thought you gave up exercising at that ritzy club when they tried to make you do interval training to a Mozart string quartet?"

"I'm not going to the club."

"Oh-h?" Linda drawled, eyeing her unusual attire. "Where, pray tell, are you going?"

"Caleb has gone to my father's studio for the afternoon. Jake has been transforming the basement into a gym at my request, and he's agreed to show me how to work out.''

"I'll just bet he has.'' Linda's eyes glittered with evident enjoyment. "One can only imagine the workout you'll receive.''

DELANEY PULLED THE JAGUAR into the driveway and killed the engine. For several seconds, she sat looking at the house, contemplating all the changes that had taken place in her life over the past few weeks.

It felt good to be in love.

Love? The word lodged in her brain, and she tried to push it away, but try as she might, it stayed there, tantalizing her. Testing her.

Did she love this man? There was no denying that she was deeply attracted to him, no denying that she found herself longing to be with him as much as possible. But was that love?

Her fingers tightened around the steering wheel just as Jake stepped into the doorway and held the screen wide.

"Hey, you!'' he called, a grin stretching across his face, his teeth flashing white. "It's about time you got home.''

Home.

Home?

Was that how he had begun to feel about her, about this place? The mere sound of his voice, and the fondness it contained, caused a tingling sensation to settle in the pit of her belly. For days now, she had been trying to deny what she wanted. Needed.

Jacob Turk.

Not just as a temporary arrangement. But for the rest of her days.

Swinging from the car, she slammed the door and moved up the walk, slowly, deliberately, knowing that with each step, her mind was becoming more decided, her body more aroused.

What had occurred between Jake and her these past few weeks had been swift as lightning, and just as disturbing. She hadn't been expecting it—in fact, she had tried her hardest to deny it. But the truth of the matter was, in the five weeks she'd known him, he had made her feel more cherished, more desirable, than any man ever had.

More loved.

He hadn't said the words, but she knew his feelings. It was there in the way he watched her with dark, brown-black eyes. It was there in the way he teased her and protected her.

When she didn't speak for some time, he regarded her with concern. "Is something wrong?"

"No." She stopped a few inches in front of him, suddenly confident, bold. "Not a thing." She laid a hand on his waist, splaying her fingers wide, testing the resiliency of the muscles she had admired for so long. "Not a damn thing."

He must have seen something in her eyes to tell him of her feelings, her delight, because he took her wrist, holding it still against him for several long moments.

"Your mother called to say the taping at your father's studio had been delayed and they wouldn't bring Caleb home until late. He's having a ball with all the puppets. We could go out, if you'd like."

She curled her hand about the arm he'd wound around her waist. "I suppose."

"Or we could stay in."

An invitation lay buried beneath those words. One she could neither deny nor refuse.

"I'd like that."

He tightened his grip ever so slightly. He dipped his head and brushed his lips over her hair, hair that had been left long and loose and tousled.

"Show me the gym?"

"Downstairs."

They spoke in intimate verbal shorthand.

He took her through the house, not bothering to turn on the lights, but leading her easily, despite the shadows. Since the staircase that led to the basement was steep, Jake went first, allowing her the luxury of studying the dark waves of his hair, the breadth of his shoulders, the tightness of his...

"Wait here."

He left her on the bottom tread, disappearing into the gloom. She heard his footsteps leading away from her, then a muted click.

A buttery light flooded one corner of the room, illuminating the gleaming metal, vinyl and iron of the exercise equipment scattered in the vaulting space.

The air was cooler down here, whispering over her shoulders in a phantom caress. She walked forward, trailing one finger over a row of free weights.

"It all looks very professional."

"My work has depended on working hard on just such equipment."

She looked at him then, really looked at him. Allowing Jake to see all her thoughts, all her yearnings.

"I believe the hard work has paid off most admirably." She slowly circled him, tracing his arm, his back, his ribs, with the same finger that had slid across the cool metal of the weights. Jake's flesh proved a stark contrast in both temperature and texture, warm, resilient, and oh, so tempting.

"What should we do now?"

She paused in front of him, tipping her head back in such a way that her hair spilled over her shoulders and down her back.

His eyes narrowed, becoming nearly black in color.

"I suppose we could stick to the original plan and lift weights."

"I suppose." Delaney didn't even pause to think of the consequences. She closed her hand around the snap of her jeans, tugging it loose. "That would probably be a good idea." She lowered the zipper, knowing her actions, although innocent in and of themselves, were not being performed in an innocent manner. Indeed, she felt a rush of pure feminine power as she realized that she could also prove to be the aggressor. She could incite him.

"It's still a little warm down here."

He nodded, but didn't speak. He was watching her, waiting to see what she would do next. Smiling the smile of Eve, she kicked off her shoes and pushed her jeans over her hips to the floor. Stepping free, she rose, watching as his eyes raked her form, taking in the pale pink bike shorts that coated her thighs like a layer of ink, the color so delicate as to nearly blend with her skin. The wrinkled hem of his tank top brushed her thighs, and she knew without a doubt that he was wondering what she wore beneath.

"I don't think I'll be needing this, do you?" she inquired, gesturing to indicate his shirt. In one swift movement, she drew it over her head, revealing the black thong brief and matching bra top she'd worn underneath.

"Hell, woman, have you been wearing that under your clothes all day?"

Jake's question was purely rhetorical, but it made her smile nonetheless. In the past, she'd firmly believed that exercise gear had become a little too revealing over the years. This evening, she revised her opinion.

"Show me what to do, Jake."

He looked at her as if she'd lost her mind.

Chuckling, she sat on one of the benches, purposely stretching her arms wide, lifting her chest up in a teasing, sensual manner. "Show me, Jake."

She grasped the extension bar, but before she could bring it into play, he stopped her with a hand on her arm.

"Delaney?" It was more than her name, more than a question.

"I really want to learn."

He wasn't listening; he was watching her closely. Ever so closely.

"I've been thinking that my arms need a little work, as well as my—"

He pulled her to her feet, hauling her against his chest and bending his head for a searing kiss. All thought of conversation flew from her head. She moaned, wrapping her arms around his neck and returning the embrace, measure for measure.

Since that night when they'd celebrated her birthday, they had kissed, caressed, but the feelings that they entertained had been nothing compared to those they shared now. A fire storm of sensation swept through Delaney's body, causing her to arch against him. She needed to feel each swell, each valley, of his body. Her hands dragged over his skin, plunging beneath the barrier of his shirt, toying with the waist of his shorts.

He drew back, dragging air into his lungs. His gaze was clearly searching, looking for what had caused her to abandon the reticence she had displayed up to this moment.

"I need you, Jake."

The words were stark, vulnerable. She hadn't meant to say them, but now that they were uttered, she couldn't deny their truth.

He remained so serious, brushing the hair away from her cheeks with his palms. "I've waited so long to hear you say that." He bent to place a tender kiss on her lips, her cheek.

"You've been very patient with me."

"You've been very adorable."

She rubbed her cheek against his chest. "Jake?"

"Mmm?"

She curled her fingers into the fabric of his shirt, wondering if she had the courage to say the words that trembled on the tip of her tongue. Yet, as the seconds ticked by, she knew she couldn't say them. He wasn't ready to hear anything about love. He might never wish to hear such things from her.

"I want to be near you."

He rubbed his hand down the length of her hair.

"I want to touch you."

He grew still.

"I want . . . to make love to you."

For several moments, her heart pounded in her throat, as he made no sort of reply. Then he drew back, eyeing her consideringly.

"I care for you very much, Delaney."

He hadn't said he loved her, but she prayed that someday he would. That he would admit he belonged with her. With Caleb. She carefully ignored the fact that in a few weeks' time he would be journeying to Washington, D.C.

"I do care for you, Delaney," he said again, when she didn't immediately respond.

She curved her lips in a faint smile. "I know that. But right now, this evening, I want more."

Slipping from his embrace, she laced her fingers between his own and drew him toward the stairs. Immediately she sensed a hesitation on Jake's part. Not because he didn't agree with her plans, but because he thought that she would regret such an action in the future.

He obviously thought she would rue the day she had invited herself into his life, into his bed. But Delaney was far more certain that she would feel no such regrets. She had thought about such an actuality many times over the past few days. It had grown increasingly difficult to spend so many hours in this man's company, knowing that she had only to reach out in order to indulge her fondest wishes.

"You don't have to do this, Delaney. You don't have to prove anything to me."

She glanced over her shoulder, still climbing the steps, still leading him irresistibly upward. "I know."

She had topped the stairs, emerging in the dusky atmosphere of the kitchen. There she paused, one tread above Jake.

The gloom painted his features with the blunt purity of pale light and soft shadow. For the rest of her life, she would remember the expression on his face. One of stark tenderness, an overwhelming passion.

She could not resist; she had to reach out and assure herself that he was real. When she cupped his cheek, he leaned into the caress, the slight stubble on his jaw deliciously abrading the hollow of her palm.

"I wish I could be everything you want me to be," Delaney whispered, the words easing from her throat before she could prevent them.

"You are."

She shook her head. "No."

"What more do you think I want?"

More than she could give.

He pressed a kiss in the center of her hand. "You are a beautiful woman."

"I'm staid."

"No. Just a little shy."

"Boring."

He made a *tsk*ing sound of reproof. "No. Simply full of mystery." His hands eased around her hips and pressed against the hollow of her back, pulling her closer to his warmth. "You also have an infinite capacity to give. You're witty, charming, and smart."

"Too damned smart sometimes," she whispered.

"No. I like the fact that you have more degrees than a university."

She stared at him in surprise.

"You knew?"

"Of course. Marlene told me."

She shook her head. "I should have known."

"It doesn't matter."

"It has, to men in the past."

He touched her chin. "But not to me."

Wrapping her arms around his neck, she squeezed her eyes closed. "Make love with me, Jake." The low, fervent plea shouldn't have come from her lips in such a wanton manner, but it did. The simple phrase fairly vibrated with her desire, her fear.

When he would have spoken, she pressed her lips to his, craving the elemental sensations of passion, wanting them to push the misgivings from her mind. The worries about the future. They would talk about it later. But not until she had this one memory. This one night.

The kiss they shared erupted in a storm of desire. Jake bent, sweeping her into his arms and carrying her into his bedroom. The first whispers of moonlight seeped through the shutters that covered his windows, painting the floor and the simple four-poster bed in bars of silver.

"I want you," he whispered.

"Yes."

"But only if you're sure about this."

"I'm sure."

He set her on the ground and cupped her face in his palms. "How did you fall into my life, Delaney McBride?"

The question caused her throat to tighten.

"I wasn't expecting you, I wasn't ready for you. Yet, here you are, an angel in disguise."

"Just a woman."

"Much more, I think."

She lifted up on tiptoe. "And you are much more than a simple man."

His brow lifted.

Delaney trailed her fingertips from his shoulder, down the swell of his chest, the sweep of his ribs, the hard contours of his stomach. Although she had caressed him in such a way before, she had never done so without inhibition. But all thought of caution seemed to have dissipated into the night around them.

"In the past few days, you've taught me things about myself that I never knew—or never wanted to know." She circled the hollow of his navel with her thumb. "Now, teach me the rest. Teach me what I need to do to please you."

From that moment on, there were no more words. Jake cupped her chin, drawing her up for his kiss. She met him halfway, closing her eyes and savoring the passion, the wanton rush of pleasure, that inundated her veins. She swept her hands over his arms, his shoulders, absorbing each swell and valley of his physique.

In time, even that wasn't enough. Whimpering slightly, she wormed her fingers beneath the hem of his shirt, breaking free from the power of his embrace only long enough to sweep the garment over his head. The heat of his skin seeped into her flesh, filling her, tantalizing her.

Bit by bit, Jake backed her toward the bed, until her knees brushed against the edge of the quilt. Then he stopped, lifting his head and studying her in the faint light.

Never had a man looked at her this way. Hungrily. Adoringly. Smiling that smile she had grown to love so much, he gently pushed her onto the mattress. Kneeling in front of her, he helped her remove her shoes, her socks. All the time, his hands roamed over her calves and up her thighs. Then he helped her to stand. Swept the bra from her breasts. Slid the shorts from her hips.

When she stood before him, bathed in nothing but the silver glow of the moon, he paused, gazing at her with such devotion, she could scarcely believe that those emotions were directed toward her. Her.

His knuckles skimmed her hair, her cheek. After one tender kiss, he eased her onto the bed, then rose to divest himself of his own clothing. She watched in awe as each article dropped to the ground. When he stood naked before her, she trembled. Trembled in anticipation, desire. Disbelief.

He lay beside her, warming her body with his own. There was no haste to his lovemaking. Indeed, he seemed to take great pleasure in kissing her shoulders, her elbows, her wrists. Then, rolling her so that she lay on her stomach, he began to trail a string of caresses across her back and down her spine.

She shivered in sheer delight, never having known that a man could affect her so completely. Soon, her body throbbed with a powerful need, one so encompassing, so wanton, that she rolled onto her back, taking him by the shoulders and urging him above her.

When his weight settled over her, she saw the intensity of his expression, the stark need, the overwhelming devotion. She ran her hands down his back, cupping the swells of his buttocks, silently begging for a release for the fever pitch of passion he had aroused in them both.

He kissed her again, hungrily, completely. Bit by bit, he eased his hand between them, testing her readiness. Then, positioning himself against her womanly flesh, he entered her, slowly. Completely.

She gasped once she had taken him completely inside her. So large, so heated. When he began to move, rocking, shifting, sliding—gradually at first, then faster and faster—she found it difficult to think at all. She could only feel. Her hands grasped the rails of his headboard as her entire being seemed to center on a pleasure so intense that it approached pain, a pleasure that grew, coalesced, then shattered into a thousand splinters of delight.

She couldn't prevent the cry that burst from her lips. When it was followed by his own moan of passion, her hands clenched in the waves of his hair.

Dear heaven, how she loved him. Loved him more than life itself. For once, the old cliché held meaning for her. As his weight settled upon her and he tucked his chin against her shoulder in an effort to catch his breath, she squeezed her eyes closed, realizing she'd made a horrible mistake in not insisting on his own admission.

Jake loved her. She knew he did.

But he would never acknowledge it.

Not until he admitted there was a hole in his heart that only she could fill.

Chapter Twelve

It was Delaney who responded to the soft peal of the doorbell. Slipping from beneath Jake's arm, she wrapped his robe around her body and hurried to the front of the house.

A sleepy little Caleb rested in her father's arms. The two of them wore matching "Monkey McBride Kiddie Show" hats and T-shirts.

"Dad, you didn't have to carry him in. I could have come to the car."

Marshall McBride's eyebrows waggled. "Not dressed like that, I hope."

She felt a tinge of heat enter her cheeks, but assured herself that her father couldn't possibly guess that she had nothing on underneath.

"Just show me where to put him, and I'll carry him to his bed."

He followed her to Caleb's room, his eyes brightening at the zoo motif she'd chosen. She'd spent two days of her vacation papering a mural of jungle leaves that parted here and there to show the heads of cartoon animals. Monkey McBride held the place of honor at the head of Caleb's bed, and the rest of the room was crowded with stuffed animals.

Once her father had set the boy in the crib, she removed Caleb's shoes, socks, overalls and shirt. Not wanting to disturb him further in order to put his pajamas on, she tucked a sheet under his chin, and put a stuffed bear within easy reach.

When she finished, it was to find her father eyeing her with an expression such as she had never seen before. One that was so nostalgic, so tender.

"You do love the boy, don't you?"

She shrugged, folding her arms. "More than I would have ever thought possible."

"What do you think will happen? Will you be given custody?"

"I don't know. Mrs. Atkinson, the attorney, seemed impressed by her last visit, but I'm sure she'll be adding a few more surprise inspections before the trial period is over. I just hope..."

"What?"

"If I'm not given Caleb's custody, he would go with Jake."

"Ah..."

"Jake is wonderful with him. Every kid should have a dad like that. I feel like such a... such a..."

"Creep?" her father suggested with a grin.

She laughed. Trust her father to handle the situation with his usual humor. "Yes."

"Then you'll need to trust the professionals to make the decision for you."

She frowned. "What do you mean?"

"A lawyer has been put in charge. She'll carefully weigh the options and put the child's welfare ahead of all other considerations. You'll have to live with whatever she decides, knowing it's all for the best."

She nodded, the emotions rising inside her much too strong to allow her to speak. Quiet edged into the room like a comfortable blanket. Her father didn't move. He merely gazed at her with the same eyes that had comforted children of all ages for over forty years.

"What else has you worried, Pumpkin?"

She opened her mouth to deny that anything was the matter, but he continued, "Is it that nanny fellow? Are things getting serious?"

"How did you know?" she breathed in astonishment. But then, her father had always had a way of uncovering whatever secrets she had, whether they were pleasant or grim.

"I met him when I came to pick up the boy."

"You came with Mother this afternoon?"

"Of course I did. I like that fellow."

"You do?" Delaney couldn't contain her surprise.

"He's got a good head on his shoulders. We compared a few battle notes, he and I, once he mentioned he was a history buff of sorts."

"That's not the half of it, Dad." Caleb made a snuffling noise, and she motioned for her father to follow her into the living room. "He restores armor and weaponry and uniforms—then makes true-to-scale patterns to recreate them for theatrical productions."

"He struck me as being very ambitious."

Which meant her father had probably given him the Inquisition-like interview he gave most men who found their way into her life.

Sighing, she sank onto the couch. "That's part of the problem."

"Oh?"

She hesitated only a moment before telling him everything. "Jake will be leaving soon. He's been given a job at some museum back east."

Marshall nodded as if he already knew. "The Smithsonian."

Delaney stared at him. She'd had no idea. She'd never even bothered to ask the details.

Shaking her head, she stared down at her hands, blinking at the moisture that threatened to spill over her lashes. "If there were more time...better circumstances..."

Her father grunted. "What makes you think any of us is given the right amount of time or the perfect circumstances when it comes to romance, Pumpkin? Your mother and I knew each other for nine years before her parents would let us consider marriage. Even then, they insisted I be able to provide her with a house and three rooms of furniture. Others—like you and your beau—get less. A week. Or two. Or three. It doesn't matter. What counts is what you make of the time you have. The sacrifices you make—on both sides."

"But I don't know if what we have..."

"Will last? Will be enough to offset the changes required? That's what love *is,* honey. A giant crapshoot. It's how much you really want things to work that counts." He cupped her cheek, forcing her to look up at him. "Do you want it to work between you?"

She nodded.

"Then do what you have to do, sweetie."

She rose, wrapping her arms around him. "Thanks, Dad."

"That's what fathers are for." He patted her back. "Just don't tell your mother. Mothers think it's *their* privilege in life to do the listening and the advising. Besides, your mother would never give you a moment's peace if she knew you had your heart tangled up with ol' Jake. She'd be dragging you down to the bridal shop before he even had a chance to pop the question."

Delaney laughed, knowing it was true. That sense of well-being stayed with her long after Mr. McBride had driven away.

Wrapping her arms around her waist, she padded back to Caleb's room—just to check on him one last time. As she was leaning close to kiss his cheek, he roused, just for a moment, and patted her nose.

"Mama," he said with a sigh.

Her heart clenched.

"Oh, I do love you, Caleb. It shouldn't have happened so quickly or so completely, but I love you with all my heart."

From the hallway, Jake heard the whispered statement. Heard it and felt a sliver of pain prick his heart as he admitted the truth he'd known for days.

He couldn't take Caleb from her now. To do so would rip his heart from his chest. But to leave him with Delaney would take more strength of will than he had ever possessed.

The squeak of a floorboard warned him of Delaney's approach, and he hurried back to the bedroom. When she entered, he was sitting amid the covers, waiting.

"You're awake," she breathed.

"Mmm-hmm . . ."

"My father just dropped Caleb off."

"That's what I figured."

She shifted from foot to foot, obviously wondering how much he'd heard.

Standing, he crossed the room, pinning her against the wall. Bending, he nibbled her ear, her jaw, then brushed his lips across hers.

"Touch me," he said, tugging at the tie of his own robe. It looked much better on her. Much more delectable.

Delaney could no longer resist. Not now. Not ever. Perhaps she would have Jake with her for only a short time. Perhaps she would have him forever. But all that mattered in this instant was the strength of his arms, the husky intoxication of his voice, and the wicked, wicked light in his eyes.

Pushing him back to the edge of the bed, she knelt in front of him, the robe gaping to provide him a healthy view of her breasts, her torso, her navel. But instead of filling her with self-consciousness as it once would have done, now it merely enflamed her, made her even more bold.

She slid her hands over his feet, his ankles, his calves. When she rubbed upward, ever upward, over his thighs, he moaned, collapsing backward onto the bed and hauling her with him for a crushing kiss.

The embers of passion that they had stirred earlier that evening exploded into a potent, overwhelming need. Delaney couldn't get enough of his taste, explore enough of his texture. She roamed her hands over his back, his shoulders, his buttocks, even as her body strained toward him.

He gasped, drawing back, stringing kisses down her jaw, her throat. "I do care for you, Delaney. More than you'll ever know."

It wasn't an avowal of love, but for now it was enough. She arched toward him, needing more of him, all of him. Her limbs soon trembled with desire. When he pressed her back against the cool sheets, she moaned, "Yes, yes," gripping his hair and wrapping her legs around his waist.

Then he was plunging inside her, filling that portion of her body which ached for his possession. She cried out, not able to control the instinctive sound of pleasure. Her fingernails bit into his skin, her teeth sank into his shoulder. She was tensing, tensing, an unbearable pleasure drawing taut in her body before it shattered into a thousand splinters of pleasure.

Later, much later, Jake held her close, stroking her hair. After a tender smile, he took the time to close the draperies against the pink light of morning before joining her.

"Jake?" she murmured, so tired, so relaxed, she could barely form the word.

"Mmm..."

"I need to tell you—"

"Shh." He drew her head against his chest and wrapped one leg over her knee. "Sleep."

"But—"

"Later, Delaney. For now, you need your sleep. Just sleep."

So somehow, amid the heaviness of her eyes and the sated thrum of her body, the opportunity to tell him how much she loved him dissipated into the shadows.

SHE SLEPT. Jake propped himself against the doorway, gazing at the woman who lay in his bed.

She was beautiful. Beautiful and vulnerable and innocent. Yet, to help her, he would have to hurt her.

He sighed, digging his hands into his pockets to keep from slamming them against the wall. He kept trying to tell himself that it didn't matter, that he didn't have the time for a relationship like this. Not now. Not yet. Not with a child to complicate things between them.

Jake knew she loved him. It was so obvious, shining from her eyes in a way that seemed to light her up from within.

But he couldn't accept that love. He couldn't even let her voice it. To do so would hurt her even more. If he stayed and she was given custody of Caleb, she would never believe he'd come to love her for herself and not for the child. She would think he was using her to stay with Caleb. Even though nothing could be further from the truth.

She loves you, the little voice in his head said again, but it seemed to be growing fainter, weaker.

Grasping the bag containing his belongings from the floor, he turned and walked out of her life.

AT NINE O'CLOCK, he met Twila Atkinson as she entered her office.

"Can I talk to you?"

Her brows rose, but only a bit.

"Of course."

Ushering him into the inner sanctum of her office, she motioned for him to sit and retrieved a file from the corner of her desk.

"Marlene Detry has put us both in a bit of a quandary," she said before he could stop her. "Frankly, I'm in hot water up to my eyeballs trying to convince the authorities that I didn't know she planned to skip the country. The fact that I did the legal legwork for the custody arrangements doesn't allow a lot of credibility for my cause." She exhaled, as if the mere speech had exhausted her. "Nevertheless, I've corresponded with Marlene by fax—via her friends, so that the FBI weren't able to trace her. She seemed genuinely concerned about her son."

"I'll bet," Jake said, unable to control the tinge of bitterness in his voice.

"She says that she trusts my judgment, so..." Twila gave him a glance worthy of a Supreme Court justice. "What do you want to do, Jake? After the way Marlene embroiled you in her little games, I figure you deserve a say in all this."

"Give custody to Delaney McBride." The words scraped against his throat as they emerged, but he had to give Twila credit for not showing her surprise.

"You're sure?"

"Yes."

"Once these things are done, it's very hard to undo them."

"I know." He stood. "She's good for him, Twila." He took a deep breath to ease the tightness in his chest. "And he's already the light of her life."

Chapter Thirteen

"That tape of yours is driving me nuts."

One of Jake's assistants, Dirk Roberts, leaned against the wooden railing of the storage loft overhead and scowled down at his companion. Jake paid little attention, reinserting the cassette in the VCR on the counter and resuming the intricate work he was doing on a chain-mail hood.

"Who is that kid, anyway?" Dirk demanded.

"His name is Caleb De—Caleb McBride."

"So why the tape?"

"It was a gift. Monkey McBride sent it to me."

"No kidding? You know Monkey McBride?" It amazed Jake that Dirk was more impressed by the kiddie-show host than by the intricate armor stored all around them.

"Even so, we've seen that same damned recording of that same damned show at least twelve damned times! Don't you think you've got it memorized by now? How about something more entertaining?''

Jake didn't even bother to respond; he merely glared at his companion and continued his work. Ever since the tape had arrived in the mail via his office, he hadn't been able to watch anything else. The sight of the little boy cavorting all over the soundstage, filmed by an obviously proud-as-punch grandfather, did nothing to ease his heartache.

But it wasn't only Caleb that made him yearn for might-have-beens. It was also the lithe, feminine woman dressed in a severe suit, her hair coiled against her nape.

Why? Why had she lost the laughter he'd become accustomed to? What had dimmed the fire in her eyes?

It couldn't be his disappearance.

Could it?

Dirk swore again and punched the eject button, retrieving the tape and holding it high above his head. "I swear, if you play it one more time, I'll kill myself.''

Jake didn't even crack a smile at the joke. Instead, he growled in a menacing voice, "Put it back.''

Dirk threw the tape onto the counter and sank into his own chair, offering Jake a look of disbelief. "What's got into you lately? You weren't like this in San Diego last year.''

The two of them had worked on a project together for a local museum. At the time, Jake had thought he'd enjoy working with the man. Now, he wasn't so sure.

Snatching the videocassette, Jake threw it into his gym bag. "It's none of your business."

"None of my business? I'm your partner, remember? Your second-in-command. So tell me, what's got you as easy to live with as a grizzly bear with a sore paw?"

"I don't want to talk about it." Jake draped the hood over a wig stand and rose to his feet. In the mirror on the opposite wall, he caught the reflection of his face. He hadn't slept much in the past few days, and it showed. More than he wanted to admit.

Dirk refused to be cowed by Jake's attitude. "Of course you don't want to talk about it—because it involves the woman in the background, doesn't it?"

Jake froze.

"Admit it. You've got something for the girl and her kid. But they're on the West Coast and you're on the East."

"It's not that simple."

"It's never simple. Not where women are involved." He shook his head. "Face it, man, you blew it. You love that woman. So much that it makes your teeth ache. But you're too damned stubborn to admit it."

"You don't know what you're talking about." Jake pushed himself upright and began his circuit again.

Dirk surveyed the path he made—a rudely formed figure eight that covered most of the narrow room. "I think I know enough—and I've watched the way you've changed over the last few weeks. You've become a royal pain in the butt. Until that tape came." He shook his head. "Never have I seen a man so crazy over a woman. You've been mooning over that tape like a teenager with his first crush."

"She doesn't need me now," Jake said. "She's got her own life. One she deserves to keep. I, on the other hand, am under contract for at least a year."

Dirk measured him with a glance. "What makes you think she wouldn't move out here?"

"The woman's got everything where she is. A home, career, recognition, honors and degrees in a list as long as my arm."

"That bothers you, huh?"

"Damn straight."

"Why?"

"Because I don't have anything at all to give her in return!"

"Don't you?" When Jake did not respond, Dirk poked him in the chest with his finger. "You must be more blind than you think, if you can't see that woman needs something. Some...lightening up. You could do that, Jake."

Jake grew still. He'd already done it. He'd made her laugh again.

"You've got a lot to offer her, if you can find the courage to admit that she does need you. Not as her superior, not as her provider, but as her equal."

"Men! We've got a staff meeting, you know!"

The call came from the hall. Before Jake could respond, Dirk said, "Think about it." Then he left, abandoning Jake to his own regrets.

It wasn't until later that he admitted Dirk had unwittingly been right. In fact, he might have continued to deny the truth, to ignore what he really wanted from life, from Delaney, except that he took the time to watch the video one last time before leaving for home.

The moment he saw that damned suit, that damned old-maidish hair, a wave of shame tumbled through him, then a surge of determination. He loved this woman. No matter what he'd said, or what she'd proclaimed, they needed one another. They were two lonely souls who were complete only in each other's arms.

He set the hood he'd been working on back on the counter and strode into the black night. So what was he going to do?

The answer didn't come to him until he arrived home. There he found an expensive vellum envelope tucked in his mailbox. It contained an invitation to a reception hosted by the Lexington Fertility and Research Institute in honor of the brilliant achievements of one Delaney McBride and three of her colleagues.

Instantly Jake knew that Delaney hadn't been responsible for sending the invitation. If he was to bet money on it, he'd guess that Dodie McBride had probably mailed it. There was a small note at the bottom explaining that she was the chairwoman.

Grinning, he kissed the envelope and rushed indoors. Finally, he knew what he had to do. He just needed to set the events in motion.

THE PARTY would be incredibly stuffy.

Delaney frowned at her own thought, stepping into the foyer of the exclusive hotel that was to hold the Lexington Institute reception and handing her invitation to the hotel employee who had been assigned to "guard" the huge gilt double doors.

Never before had she had such a reaction to one of these affairs. True, she had never been totally enamored of the events, but in the past she'd been patient, accepting that attending them was part of her job—especially when her mother was responsible for their creation.

But tonight, as she stood at the head of the shallow steps leading into the ballroom, she wondered why she hadn't manufactured an excuse to avoid this evening. Her eyes swept over the glittering crowd that had assembled, noting the women in their exquisite ball gowns, the men in their tuxedos.

Only weeks before, she had thought to bring Jake with her, to introduce him to her friends. How could she have possibly entertained the idea? With his long hair and powerful body, he would have looked and felt distinctly out of place. He would have hated her for insisting he come. He would have called it "stuffy" or "staid."

Turning resolutely away from that assumption, she realized it was only one more reason to add to the dozens she had already formed about why his sudden departure was for the best. She must have suffered a momentary aberration, to think she belonged with such a man. She was part of *this* circle of people. Those who had more money and brains and decorum than the rest of the world thought proper. Those who refused to drop their guard long enough to entertain the frivolities of life.

"Good evening, Delaney." Dodie sidled up beside her, taking her elbow and ushering her down into the sea of guests. Thankfully, she hadn't worn the toga from her credit card advertisement, but was dressed instead in a stunning beaded caftan that made her look like the embodiment of the social butterfly she was.

"It's about time you got here, dear," Dodie commented once they were out of earshot of the board of directors, who waited near the doors as an informal welcoming committee.

Her father peered at her from beneath bushy brows. "You're usually so prompt at these events. Yet here you are, nearly a half hour late."

Delaney didn't bother to explain the truth. Her only comment was "The traffic was awful."

Dodie made a sound of disbelief. "Yes, and my aunt Rita plays basketball for the Lakers."

A waiter passed them bearing a tray of champagne, and Delaney defiantly took a glass.

Dodie's brow lifted. "My, my, my... I don't think I've ever seen you drink anything harder than lemonade."

"I seem to have developed a taste for wine." Red wine, ribs, fried chicken...

Her mother only smiled. "Stunning dress. It's a little more... daring than your last one, isn't it?"

Delaney refused to be baited into responding. Little did Dodie know. Delaney had bought the midnight-blue creation with Jake in mind. It had been meant to be a surprise. A sort of comment on her transformation over the past few months. The filmy chiffon skirt fell from her waist to the floor, skimming her limbs and offering a purely sensual effect, despite its simple cut. Above, a modest brocade jacket of blue and gold hugged her body, coyly teasing about the curves to be found beneath. The costume would have been completely proper—nearly staid—if not for the fact that the jacket hid a stunning bustier of sequins, pearls and rhinestones that hugged her torso and pushed her breasts upward in a manner she knew no man could ignore. Added to that was the fact that the garment allowed little more in the way of underwear than...

Than a merry widow, panties, a garter, and silk stockings.

She clenched her jaw a little tighter together. Tonight, the revealing portions of the gown would remain hidden. Another sign of how Jake's rejection had thrust her back into the world where she belonged. One that was overly concerned with social proprieties. Reserved.

Boring.

Dodie took one look at the crease between her brow and laughed. "So what has you all grumpy tonight? Was Caleb difficult about having a sitter?"

"No. Kim lives next door. She brought her little sister to play with him."

"Then what's put you in such a foul mood? Could it be the result of the terminated alliance between you and Mr. Turk?"

Delaney shot her another warning glance. "Leave it alone, Mother. It has nothing at all to do with Jake."

Dodie's eyes sparkled. "Well, then, you probably wouldn't be interested in the fact that he just stepped through the door."

She laughed softly when Delaney froze in stunned surprise. "Enjoy yourself, sweetie." Then she backed away, joining another group of people conversing near the buffet table.

The moment she left, Delaney felt a tingling up her spine, one she had felt before. Bit by bit, she pivoted toward the source.

There at the head of the stairs was one of the most beautiful creatures she had ever laid her eyes on. Jacob Turk. He was dressed splendidly in a black cut-away tuxedo, white vest, white shirt, white tie. The austere combination only served to intensify his own dramatic coloring. He looked sophisticated, polished—except for the waves of his hair that hung, unbound, midway down his back, giving him an almost primitive air.

The gasps of a few of the guests caused a ripple of silence to spread throughout the room. All eyes turned to the stranger who had just entered. It was obvious that they wondered why he was here and who he could possibly be. A few might have recognized him as the man who had whisked Delaney so precipitately out of the institute's parking lot weeks before. But since a majority of those gathered were from the governing and scientific board, most had no prior knowledge of Jacob Turk.

Jake purposely waited until he had everyone's attention. Then, moving with that sinuous grace she was beginning to believe was his trademark, he handed his invitation to the waiting attendant and descended the shallow steps leading into the ballroom. At the bottom, he paused, ever so slightly, looking at Delaney, studying her, making it obvious to all that he had come to this gathering because of her.

She became immediately conscious of the severity of her hair, the artful makeup, the body-covering gown. Something flickered deep in his eyes, something that appeared very much like sadness. Then his lips tilted in what looked like satisfaction and he altered his course, heading toward the orchestra that filled the room with the strains of a muted samba. Whispering in the bandleader's ear, he slipped him a tip and pivoted, his gaze immediately returning to Delaney.

A rush of anticipation flooded her body, but she fought to ignore it. She didn't know why he was here. She tried to tell herself that it probably had nothing to do with her, nothing to do with the way he watched her so keenly.

But when he began to move toward her, she had no illusions, no thought that he'd come on behalf of another woman. His eyes glittered purposefully, causing her heart to beat a little faster, her mouth to grow dry. She only prayed he wouldn't choose this night, this occasion, to toy with her. If she had to say goodbye again, her heart would break.

A desperation filled her breast. A potent yearning. Suddenly, she realized she would do anything to keep him—give away her money, resign from her job—if only he would find a way in his heart to live with a woman like her.

Within seconds, the samba had been concluded. A strange silence cloaked the ballroom. Every scrap of attention seemed trained upon the two of them, and she knew the guests must wonder what this exotic-looking man wanted with the reclusive Delaney McBride.

He stopped a few feet away, holding out his hand. At the same time, the band began to play a sensual rock ballad, the one she and Jake had danced to at Adam's Ribs. That night he'd broken down her reserve. That night he'd held her in his arms. That night when their relationship had become personal.

"I've come to claim a dance," he murmured for her ears alone.

She looked around her, wondering what sort of gossip would be circulating within minutes of such an entrance. But Jake hadn't finished.

"Not just for this evening," he continued, "but for the rest of our lives. If you're willing."

Several members of the audience must have heard him because they gasped. A twittering of voices ebbed toward the corners of the room as the news was passed along to those who were too far away to understand what was happening.

The music flowed over them, and Jake took her into his arms, swaying to the beat, folding her close to his heart. Leaning near to her ear, he murmured, "I'm also here to confess that I had a chance to make Caleb my own responsibility. But I couldn't take him away from you. I wouldn't. So I left, thinking that if I stayed, you would think I was using you to get to the boy. But now I've discovered that I can't live without *you*, Delaney McBride.

"I want to marry you. I want to wake up seeing you first thing in the morning and go to bed with you last thing at night. I want to grow old with you, so that in fifty or sixty years we can rock together on the porch and say, 'Look what we've done together.' I want you to become my wife, my partner, and my companion—and if Caleb is thrown in with the bargain, that's just a bonus.''

Delaney's heart was beating so hard she felt sure that Jake could hear it. She could scarcely believe the words he spoke, the avowals of love made in the midst of hundreds of people—and yet privately expressed. Intimately spoken.

"I need you, Delaney," he whispered huskily, leading her easily through the other dancers who had joined them on the floor. "I need the happiness you bring me, I need your wit, your charm. I need you to keep my feet on the ground and my head in the clouds. If you say yes, I'll cherish you always and never forget that it's because of you that I'm the man I am today—as well as the better man I'll be tomorrow. In exchange, I promise to give you love, I promise to give you laughter. I promise to give you joy.''

Sudden tears rose in her eyes. When he drew back, he must have seen them, because he stopped, reaching into his pocket and withdrawing a tiny box. Opening it to reveal an exquisite, emerald-cut diamond, he smiled tenderly in her direction. "Will you be my wife, Miss Delaney McBride, child prodigy, scientist, the love of my life?''

The words were like a balm to her battered soul, infusing her with a honeyed sweetness like none she had ever known before. The room grew hushed again as those around them became aware of what was happening. A few of the occupants stopped their swaying, but others continued to dance, looking their way with fond regard.

Delaney could have cried with joy. Unconsciously, Jake was admitting not only to her, but to everyone in this room, that he loved her. But more than that, he was admitting that he'd found something he could give her in return. The emotional support, the laughter, the closeness she had craved all her life.

He was also admitting he needed her. Not her diplomas, not her degrees, not her money or her family connections. He needed her because she made him happy.

As she smiled tremulously and nodded, she knew that there was still much to be said, still much to be explained. There was the matter of their jobs and the continent between them. But for now, they had found a way to blend their worlds together, to complement one another. They were two lonely souls who had found heart mates, two loners in the world who had found companions. Without their combined forces, they would simply exist, without joy, without whimsy—and, as Jake had taught her, every life needed a little whimsy.

Jake's hand was warm and strong as he slid the ring over her finger and kissed it there. Around her, the music wove its rhythm into her soul, filling her with all the hopes for tomorrow that she had never dared to dream. Smiling, she turned and beckoned to Dodie. Amid the astonished, gaping mouthed regard of her employers and colleagues at the Lexington Institute, she slid the brocade jacket from her shoulders, revealing the strapless, backless affair that lay hidden beneath. Lifting her hands to her hair, she withdrew the sparkling pins one by one, allowing the tresses to drape around her shoulders in silken disarray.

Jake's eyes flamed, brimming with a molten satisfaction.

"Yes, Jake. I will be your wife."

The answer slipped easily from her lips, sealing her future. The crowd discreetly applauded, the silence disintegrating as they began to converse among themselves, discussing all that had occurred in the past few minutes.

But Delaney didn't care. Let them talk as much as they wanted.

Taking Jake's hand, she allowed him to draw her onto the dance floor, absorbing the strength of his hands, the intensity of his gaze.

"You might live to regret this," he murmured, but it was obvious from the dark warmth of his eyes that he doubted it.

"I'll never regret it."

"I've got to stay in Washington for at least a year."

"I don't care. I'm sure I could transfer to one of Lexington's sister centers."

"I don't ever want you to think that I came back for Caleb."

"No. I know you didn't."

He grinned. "I *do* love you. More than life itself."

"I know."

As their mouths met and the passion flared anew, she smiled. How she adored this man! His moods, his humor, his commitment. Their marriage would have its challenges—its challenges and its overwhelming triumphs. But through it all, they could only grow closer. They had already learned one important lesson. That if they were apart, they were vulnerable to life's upsets. But together...

Together they were indomitable.

Ending the kiss, Jake grinned and began to dance, drawing her hips close, twining his legs with her own. Delaney basked in it all. She would never forget this night, the emotions, the simmering desire. She would never forget the way he'd publicly claimed her. She would never forget his strength. Nor would she forget, that from this moment until the end of her days...

Caleb's Nanny Jake would be the one man in the world who had the power to leave her breathless.

Harlequin Romance ®

AVAILABLE IN OCTOBER—A BRAND-NEW COVER DESIGN FOR HARLEQUIN ROMANCE

Harlequin Romance has a fresh new eye-catching cover.

We're bringing you an exciting new cover design, but Harlequin Romance is still committed to bringing you warm and contemporary love stories that are sure to touch your heart!

See how we've changed and look for these fabulous stories with a brand-new look:

#3379 Brides for Brothers
by Debbie Macomber
#3380 The Best Man
by Shannon Waverly
#3381 Once Burned
by Margaret Way
#3382 Legally Binding
by Jessica Hart

Available in October,
wherever Harlequin books are sold.

Harlequin Romance®—
Dare To Dream

HRNEW

HARLEQUIN®
AMERICAN ◆ ROMANCE®

"Whether you want him for business...or pleasure, for one month or for one night, we have the husband you've been looking for. When circumstances dictate the need for the appearance of a man in your life, call 1-800-HUSBAND for an uncomplicated, uncompromising solution. Call now.
Operators are standing by...."

1♥800 HUSBAND

Pick up the phone—along with five desperate singles—and enter the Harrington Agency, where no one lacks a perfect mate. Only thing is, there's no guarantee this will stay a business arrangement....

For five fun-filled frolics with the mate of your dreams, catch all the 1-800-HUSBAND books:

Coming to you only from American Romance!

HFH-1

Their idea of a long night is a sexy woman and a warm bed—not a squalling infant!

To them, a "bottle" means champagne—not formula!

But Matt Hale and Ben Cooper are about to get a rude awakening. They're about to become

Join us next month for a very special duet, as Matt and Ben take the plunge into fatherhood.

Don't miss

#607 DADDY CHRISTMAS by Cathy Gillen Thacker

and

#608 MOMMY HEIRESS by Linda Randall Wisdom
Available November 1995

You've never seen daddies like these before!

Malia Rose	Chelsea Annabel	Garrett Joseph
2:32 a.m.	9:59 a.m.	12:21 p.m.
7 lbs 2 oz	8 lbs	6 lbs 12 oz

Born September 23, 1995
Riverview Hospital
Heron Point, OR

All three babies—and all
three mommies—are just fine!

Malia, Chelsea and Garrett are sure to bring change into their moms' lives—
but these special babies are about to bring them unexpected love, too!

Don't miss best-loved American Romance author Muriel Jensen's "newborn"
miniseries

MOMMY ON BOARD (October)
MAKE WAY FOR MOMMY (November)
MERRY CHRISTMAS, MOMMY (December)

Look for all the "MOMMY AND ME" books—only from Muriel Jensen
and American Romance!